BELINDA WHITE

Un-Familiar Magic

Accidental Familiar Book 3

Chapter 1

So, as it turns out, I'm a Light Witch.

You know all those years growing up thinking that my family's magical legacy had passed me by? Well, all those years past I'd been wrong. Dead wrong. Now, if I'm not careful, I'll just be plain dead too.

When I asked my family why they were so adamant about the witches' council not knowing my new status, I didn't much care for their answers. It seems that on the rare occasion when a Light Witch is unearthed, the council only has two ways to go about dealing with them. According to Lily, the first way is to put the witch, innocent or no, into a magic draining box for life. Oh, they might try to make it a fairly comfortable box, but it would be a box all the same.

Any sane person might ask why they would take such drastic measures against a witch that might have been living her life within the letter and spirit of the witches' creed, like me. The short answer is that Light Witches have an enormous amount of power. We already knew that. Some of the things I'd done since coming into my power had been nothing less than miracles. But according to the council and all their vast wisdom, that much power left to the designs of a single person is a menace to society.

Plus, and I'm sure the council portrays this as merely a side benefit to keeping society at large safe from the Light Witch, all that magic that is drained from the witch can then be put to better use by those in charge. Namely, of course, the council.

Seems awfully coincidental to me. But, of course, the council has the best interests of all witches at large. Yeah, right. Not if you happen to be a Light Witch.

So, what happens when the Light Witch protests her life sentence? Well, that's when the second way the council has of dealing with them comes into play.

They kill them.

Some choice, huh? Either live out the rest of your life in a box serving as a battery for the council's purposes or... die.

My plan? I would do just what Opal and the rest of my family advised me to do. Keep my head down, keep my emotions in check, and learn how to control this incredible power the Goddess had decided to bestow upon me.

Personally, I wish she'd chosen some other witch.

But I've been told we have to live by the cards we are dealt in life. If my life's magical card was a possible death sentence, there wasn't much I could do to change that. But I could try with all my might to keep that fact out of the hands of the witches' council.

My family and friends are trying to help.

They're also driving me more than a little crazy.

"Amie, you're tensing up. You're thinking about the council again, aren't you?" Mom's voice sounded a tad bit annoyed. With good reason, most likely. I wasn't the best of students when it came to this meditation thing.

I doubled down and forced my shoulders to drop and really tried to clear my mind. It's hard to do with the whole possible death sentence hanging over my head, but I tried. Even Mom admits, grudgingly, that I am getting better at this. It's just taking me longer than most to master it.

"That's better. Let your mind empty and just concentrate on your breathing. Breathe in one-two-three, hold one-two-three, and breathe out one-two-three." She repeated that last part until she was satisfied that I was where I needed to be. In a relaxed state. Then she went on to the next part.

"See your sanctuary up ahead. It's waiting for you. Take the two remaining steps up to it and cross the strength-giving threshold. As you do so, a soft white light surrounds you, cleansing your aura and giving you peace of mind. You are safe here. Safer than anywhere else in the universe."

I tried to push the thought out of my head that her words weren't actually true, as the place only existed in my mind. Maybe that was enough. I took the two mental steps and was a little surprised when the sensation of the light hitting my skin covered me with a gentle heat. That was... nice.

I'd put a lot of work into my sanctuary, just as Mom had instructed me to. I felt comfortable here. And yes, even safe.

It was a small glass room in the middle of the forest. With the sunlight filtering in through the leaves outside and through the glass, it would be warm in here even in the coldest of weather. I tried not to think about how hot it would be in the summer, if the little domed room actually existed. That didn't really matter, anyway, as my sanctuary was stuck in time as well as place. Perpetual spring.

Crossing the small, peaceful space, I sat on the big, fluffy bean bag chair of my youth. The one that Yorkie Doodle had destroyed during her puppy stage in real life. I loved that chair.

As I settled into its deep, soft fluffiness, the last of the tension faded away.

"Amie, wake up." Mom wasn't amused.

I'd fallen asleep again. Apparently, that wasn't supposed to happen. Unfortunately, when my body reaches that stage of almost perfect relaxation, that's what it does. Sleeps.

I sighed and opened my eyes. "Sorry, Mom. I'm not sure I'll ever get the hang of this, but I am trying."

She blew out a breath. "I know you are." She shook her head. "We'll try again tomorrow. Practice. This is important. It just might save your life one day."

How many people could say that? That meditation might save their life? It was true with me though. If what Mom said was true, anyway. Meditation strengthened the mental muscles and allowed us to call on peace of mind even in the darkest of times. Peace of mind should help me combat the magic when it came flooding in when crisis struck. Which, here lately in my life, had seemed to happen more frequently.

Hopefully, fate would give me a few years to recuperate and get my magic under control before throwing me and my family another curveball. One could only hope.

I followed Mom to the top of the inside stairs and watched as she walked down them. All of this was weighing heavily on her, I knew. She wasn't normally the hard taskmaster she'd been of late. Usually, she was as happy and carefree as anyone I'd ever known. An eternal optimist, that's my mom. The current situation had changed that.

That, in part, was the reason I was trying so dang hard to do this.

When Mom reached the bottom of the stairs, I took a deep breath and turned back into my apartment. And almost had a heart attack when I saw Ruby standing right behind me.

Sometimes I really wished Arc had never taught her that quiet shoes spell. She really took advantage of it to sneak up on me now. Maybe I should put a bell on her or something.

But then, knowing Ruby, she'd put a quiet spell on that too. It wasn't good on my already stressed out nerves.

"How'd it go today?"

I stuck my tongue out at her. Within reason, she already knew. Why should today be any different from the past week? She knew I had a long way to go on my journey to peace of mind and personal transformation.

"That good, huh?" Her smile brightened. "Well, I've got something that might help you relax a bit with all the goings on of late."

All I could do was stare at her. Like the others, she really didn't get it. Part of the reason I was so tense all the time was that everyone around me was trying to get me to relax. Kind of hard to put something out of your mind when people kept referring to it in an around about way.

"Oh, goodie."

Ruby didn't even bat a single eyelash at my bland remark. Instead, her smile turned into an outright grin. "Oh, you're gonna like this one, I think. Close your eyes."

Surprises? What was she thinking?

She gave me a not-so-light fist jab to the shoulder. "Just trust me, okay? Now, close those peepers."

Why not? After all, it was Ruby. If I couldn't trust her, who could I trust?

I felt myself being led into my living room area. I was kind of surprised when she stopped there. I'd just been in there two minutes ago. That actually kind of relieved me. It must be a small surprise. I could handle those better.

5

"Okay, you can open them now."

I did. And then I blinked.

"How… where…?"

The problem was that I couldn't believe what was now sitting where my old easy chair had been. If I hadn't known better, I'd have sworn it was the very same tie-dye looking fluffy beanbag chair that I'd loved so much, so very many years ago. That wasn't possible, though, as this chair looked like it had its stuffing intact.

In fact, it looked brand new.

"Do you like it?" Ruby was bouncing on the balls of her quiet feet.

I had to swallow the lump out of my throat. Part of the deal with sanctuaries is that they are different for every single person. They are extremely personal places for you, and maybe some figment of your imagination that you might ask to drop by for a chat. The point being, no one knew that I had this chair in my sanctuary.

How could she have possibly known? This had to be Goddess-driven. But none of that mattered, anyway.

Crossing the room only took a few steps, and I ran a hand lovingly over the soft fluff that covered the chair. "Like it? No," I said. "I love it! How did you find this?"

She grimaced. "It wasn't easy, believe me. But it was worth it." Then the color rose in her cheeks. "Don't feel too special, though. I got me one too."

I could feel the tears blurring my vision. "Thank you, Ruby. This… helps." How awesome would it be to meditate and visit my sanctuary while sitting in the same chair? Kind of a bridge from my mental state to my physical one. I couldn't wait until tomorrow's session to try it out.

Chapter 2

After spending a few minutes wallowing in my awesome new chair, I decided a trip to the library was in order. Right now, I had a lot of time on my hands, as my family was pretty adamant about me not taking on any bounty hunting jobs until we got this under control.

Not that I doubted their wisdom on that point. Sounded like a smart plan to me.

With my new chair and unusually abundant free time, I could use a few books to read. It was definitely time to visit my good friend Mabel at the Wind's Crossing Public Library.

As long as I was back by three, I was golden. I was trying really hard to not think about that three o'clock deadline and what it meant. But the thoughts crept in as I rode my bike into town, anyway.

Opal had decided to keep the store closed for a couple more weeks and to join in on my training. Mom was in charge of the meditation part—no way could I relax that much with Opal in the same room. Plus, it was kind of Mom's specialty. Opal's specialty was potions and spell casting.

That's what we were doing this afternoon. Making a potion. Opal, in her infinite wisdom, had decided that if I had this kind of power, it would be a waste not to put it to good use.

Personally, I think this whole idea stemmed from the fact that there were potions and spells that had befuddled even her magic before now. She was hoping to draw on my power to change that.

I was okay with that for the most part. It was all part of leveling up as a witch. The only odd thing about it all was the fact that I'd be helping her as much as she was helping me. No easy spells like free-lock or find. Not today, anyway. Hopefully, I could get Ruby to teach me those in some of our spare time. They could be really useful once I got back to work.

As I got closer to my destination, the shouting started to register in my brain. Oh, Goddess. Crazy Al was back at it again. Sure enough, as I turned down the little side road to the library's main entrance, I saw him standing on his milk carton across the street.

He'd tried to take up residence on the steps of the library a time or two, but Clarence had put an end to that pretty quickly. At least this way, patrons didn't have to get within arm's reach of the man. Not that he was dangerous.

More… dedicated, I guess you'd say.

"We have to take back our town," he yelled. "Drive out the wife beaters, drug dealers, and child molesters. It's time for the good men to show themselves and come forth to do God's work…" He rambled on, but I lost interest pretty fast. It was the same thing every day he showed up to preach. He was trying to raise an army of men to right the wrongs of Wind's Crossing.

Funny, but I thought we already had one. It was called the Sheriff's Department.

The library didn't seem to be all that busy, but I still hesitated to go in. Even if it would get me out the vocal range of Crazy

Al.

Most of that hesitation came from the fact that Tommy Hill's motorbike was parked at the curb out front. He and I were at that awkward stage right now, seeing as how his mom had tried to kill all us Ravenswinds. And how he'd confessed his crush on me too.

We'd both decided that wouldn't work out. It would break whatever tiny little thread was still holding Naomi Hill together. Hence, the awkward part.

In the end, I just sucked it up, took a deep breath, and went in.

He was standing at the circulation desk deep in conversation with Mabel. I took note when I heard her giggle. Mabel wasn't generally the giggling schoolgirl type. But then maybe she didn't normally have a hot geek leaning on her counter talking her up.

I strode over to them. "Hey, guys, what's so funny? I could use a good laugh right about now."

Instead of an immediate answer, my friends blushed. Both of them. That was odd.

"Nothing really, just a funny thought I had about books," Tommy said after the brief silence. He looked over at Mabel and gave his little lopsided smile. "I'd better get back to work. See you later." Then he nodded at me and left.

I tilted my head at Mabel. We'd been friends for a while. "Spill."

She lifted a shoulder and wouldn't meet my eyes. "Nothing to spill. I'm going through a hard time with Ralph, and Tommy was just trying to cheer me up."

Sounded like it was working too. But I hated to hear about the Ralph part.

"What's Ralph up to now?" When she didn't answer right away, I continued. "You know there's plenty of room at the farmhouse if you need it."

She nodded, still avoiding my eyes. I didn't like that one bit. Maybe I should take the time out of my schedule to go and have a little talk with Ralph. Then I thought about my new, emotion controlled—or rather uncontrolled—magic and decided that might not be such a good idea after all.

"So, what do you recommend I read until the next Stephanie Plum book comes out?" If she wasn't ready to talk, then changing the subject would do us both a favor.

Mabel swallowed, then smiled at me. "How do you feel about witch mysteries?"

I blinked at her. "You have those?" I mean, where'd they been all my life?

She laughed, not a giggle, but it was still good to hear from her. "Yes. They're quite popular these days. Taking over the online book stores right now." She glanced over her shoulder, but her single co-worker was far enough away to not have heard her. "Not that I'm recommending you get an eReader or anything like that. I like you coming in here."

So did I. Besides, I loved the feel of a book of my hand. Still, the thought of not having to ride my bike a few miles to get reading material had its pluses. Might be something to look into.

Mabel jotted a few names down for me to check out, and I headed off into the stacks in search of them. The next hour went by fast. The witch mysteries sounded hilariously fun. It was entertaining to read what the ordinary human world thought of us. If a single one of these authors was an actual witch, I'd be surprised. They probably still thought we were mythical creatures or something.

Not the human variety of witch, of course. Everyone knew those existed. But the magical kind, like my family? Yeah, people didn't really want to think about us being in the same world as them. Power is scary when it's in someone else's hands.

I got that. That was part of the reason I found Aunt Opal so scary. Now that I had power of my own... well, okay, so that really hadn't changed things. Opal was still scary.

When I had all the books I thought it safe to put in my bike's basket, I made my way to the checkout. Mabel was busy checking in the books from the outside drop, so I waited. It wasn't as if I was in any hurry. If I got home too soon, Opal might decide to start the spell lesson a bit earlier. The longer I could put that off, the better.

With Mom back in residence, at least temporarily, dinner times were back to being extremely punctual. That meant the lesson would be over no later than six o'clock. Surely, I could handle three hours.

When Mabel finally turned to me, I gave her a bright smile. I wasn't about to bring up the subject of Ralph again. If she wanted to talk about it, she knew I would be willing to listen. That's what good friends did.

"I see you found some." She grinned at me. "Since I'm the one that recommended them to you, I really hope you like them."

"Hey, they combine two of my favorite topics, what wouldn't I like about that?"

She shook her head. "I'm pretty sure the authors don't really understand how the real-life witch thing works." She wrinkled her nose. "I hope that doesn't upset you."

"It would upset me more if the authors did know and exposed

us to the world. I like things the way they are."

Mabel considered that for a minute and then gave me a short nod. "I think you might be right about that. A person might be smart, but in general people are..."

"Stupid." We finished it together. It was an old saying that we loved. Meaning of course, that any single person might be intelligent and understanding, but get enough people in a group and things could get ugly quick. Just look at politics.

"You're going to need a bag for these," she said, reaching up to the top shelf to bring one down. When she did, the stretching movement caused her short top to ride up just enough for me to see the large bruise underneath.

I couldn't hold it in any longer. Not after seeing that.

"Did Ralph give you that bruise?"

She whirled around and tugged the top down, shaking her head. "Just me being clumsy."

I didn't need Ruby's truth spell to know she was lying. But what could I say? Maybe it was time for me to pay a visit to Ralphie boy after all. If my magic was going to hurt someone, I couldn't think of a better person to turn it loose on.

The sight of that bruise and its implication of exactly the kind of man Ralph was had me more than a little distracted. I almost ran right into Billy Myers as he was coming into the library. It was a little like running into a brick wall. Or, a more accurate description, running into a wall of pure, hard muscle.

He put a hand out to steady me. If he hadn't, I probably wouldn't have stopped until I reached the bottom of the library's stone steps. And I wouldn't have been on my feet at the bottom.

"Thanks, Billy."

"No problem." He looked past me into the library. "Are they

busy today?"

"As far as I know I was the only patron in there, and I'm leaving." Then curiosity got the better of me. "Why do you ask?"

He blushed. "Ms. Mabel is teaching me how to read better. She's real patient, and I'm already up to the Hardy Boys books. She says if I keep practicing, I'll be ready for the Black Stallion books soon." He ducked his head. "I really like horses. I'm hoping to read them this summer."

"Then I'm sure you will, Billy. You're a pretty smart guy, you know?"

He gave a short laugh. "Maybe at building things and stuff, but not book learning smart." He took a deep breath. "I really owe Ms. Mabel for helping me." He shrugged. "Everyone else just kind of wrote me off. Not her."

Yeah, Mabel was good to her friends.

She just had lousy taste in husbands.

Chapter 3

I stood on the sidewalk for a few minutes, debating my next step. Luckily, I could do so in silence as Crazy Al must have been taking a break. I didn't want to hesitate too long, though, because his milk crate was still there. He wouldn't leave it for long.

As much as I wanted to pay Ralphie a visit of the witchy variety, I knew in my heart that wouldn't be a wise thing to do. If I blew it now, the council would have me for sure.

But that didn't mean I would sit around and do nothing when my friend was in trouble. Heck, no.

The sheriff's station was only a few doors down, so I decided to hoof it, instead of having to mess with my bike lock. Not having a car had been a mere inconvenience back before I'd ever had one. Now, it seemed a much more dire situation. I was really hoping the insurance company kept their promise, and I got that check from them tomorrow.

My eyes had almost bugged out when they'd told me the amount they were sending me. At first, I thought I'd made out like a bandit. Then I'd looked around at some used car lots. Yeah, not so much. I could get a ride for the insurance payout, but it wasn't going to be anything as nice as my precious Challenger. The only plus was that this one wouldn't be an affront to women everywhere with nasty slogans and symbols all over it.

Goddess, but I missed that car.

Squaring my shoulders, I started walking. Walking was good for me. I should probably join a gym or something. Even that short time period that I'd had my baby had made me soft. I couldn't afford that.

All the eyes in the station rose as I walked in. The station house and jail were all one big, interconnected building. You could get in the front door, but if you wanted to get behind the bullet-resistant glass, you had to ring the buzzer.

Unless your boyfriend saw you first and opened the door for you.

Opie grinned at me. "This is a surprise." Then he paused. "It's a nice surprise, isn't it? You didn't get into trouble, did you?"

I just looked at him. "No, I'm not in trouble, but I need to talk to you about Mabel."

His look sobered instantly, and he led me over to his desk. Opie was, in my opinion, the best deputy the sheriff had. It wasn't normal for him to be on desk duty, but until they released him from medical care over the buckshot wounds he'd taken to his leg while trying to protect me and my family, well, desk duty it was.

He sat at a station which was surprisingly clean. The surrounding ones were covered in paperwork. I raised an eyebrow at him.

"No, I'm not goofing off. I should be back on regular duty in a day or two. I'm trying hard to convince the doc to finally sign off on my release. I think he will after my next visit."

That was good news. Kind of, anyway. I worried about him.

Having an officer of the law as a boyfriend was hard on the nerves. It was a good thing that Wind's Crossing didn't have many serious criminals. Just a few nutcases.

I wasn't even going to think about how hard it was having a Light Witch as a girlfriend. Of course, neither of us had known about that when we'd upgraded our relationship status from best friends.

His finger was tracing the sheriff star on his desk pad calendar over and over. Finally, he looked back up at me. "Look, about Mabel…" Then he trailed off.

"Yes, about Mabel. Well, really about Ralph. Did you know he hit her?"

He wouldn't look me in the eyes. He knew.

"Half the town knows what goes on behind their closed doors, Amie. But there isn't anything we can do about it until either he messes up and does it with a witness around, or she makes a formal complaint. Neither of which has happened yet."

"So, we just sit around and do nothing?" That couldn't be right.

Opie squirmed in his chair. "It goes against my grain, too, believe me. But from the side of the law, there isn't anything I can do." Then he realized what he'd said. Maybe it was the calculating look on my face. "And don't you go doing anything, either."

When a couple of people looked our way at his slightly panicked tone, he lowered his voice. "Promise me you won't do anything to Ralph."

I considered and then shook my head. Here's the thing. I believe in the power of promises. It might be a witch thing, but if you wanted to keep your life going in the right direction, you kept the promises you made. This wasn't one I felt comfortable making.

Someone had to do something. Mabel didn't deserve this.

"Look, I'm not telling you not to do anything. Talk to Mabel. Try to convince her to call us the next time an incident occurs. Or better yet, try to get her to leave the jerk. But Ralph himself is off limits." He glanced around and lowered his voice even further. Practically a whisper. "You can't draw attention to yourself right now, and you know it."

I glared at him, but yeah, I knew he was right. It would be incredibly stupid of me to draw attention to myself by taking Ralph on.

But then, I'm not particularly known for my intelligence.

I was starting to think Crazy Al might not be so crazy after all.

* * *

I turned onto the driveway to the farmhouse at five minutes till three. How's that for timing? I'm a master at procrastination.

But when I saw the white van parked out front, I regretted taking my time. We had visitors. Lily had come to call. If I was really lucky, she'd be here for a reason—to help with the spelling lesson.

I stashed my bike in the little lean-to and headed inside. Everyone was gathered in Mom's living room. She'd done a good job of getting it all fixed up after the whole firebomb thing. The new furniture was nice. Even more comfortable than what she'd had before. And that was saying something.

"Hey, Lily, you here to join me and Opal for some potion brewing?"

The hope must have come through in my voice. Or maybe it was the desperation. Either way, she laughed.

"As a matter of fact, yes. Or, well, not with potion brewing. That really isn't my specialty. Opal asked me to come and help the two of you establish the threshold wards that I have on my house." She paused, looking me in the eyes. "That particular ward takes a lot of power. It took me and the Minehearts three days to get it down on all my windows and doors."

She didn't have to go on. This would be yet another test of just how powerful I was. I got that now. But if the end result was a home that no one bad could walk into, that was fine by me. I couldn't think of a better use for my power.

Well, if you didn't count ending a low-life named Ralph. But that would have to wait.

"Are you joining us too, Mom?"

Mom met my eyes, and I could tell I wasn't going to like what she was about to say.

"Actually, dear, I'm heading back to Oak Hill tonight."

There, see, I was right. I had really been enjoying having Mom back home. If you didn't count the times when she was driving me crazy with the whole meditation thing.

Of course, with her no longer in residence, maybe I'd catch a break on the whole peace of mind training bit. I had to admit, that part of it sounded kind of nice. And it wasn't like Oak Hill was all that far away.

Now that I knew where she was, I could visit her whenever I wanted. That would be much easier once the insurance company came through with that check. On a bike, her new town might as well be on the moon.

"Don't worry, sweetie, I've made arrangements with Ruby to continue your meditation training."

Dang, I just couldn't catch a break. But what I said was, "Oh, good."

She gave me a big hug and then the same to Opal. I was kind of surprised when Opal returned it. My aunt wasn't usually the affection-showing type. But then, the last few weeks had been hard on all of us. Maybe I wasn't the only one that had changed.

We all walked Mom out to her car and saw her off. Then Lily and Opal turned to me.

"Let's see how this goes, shall we?" Lily asked.

I took a deep breath and nodded. It wasn't like I really had a choice in the matter, now was it?

They had already laid out all the necessary ingredients to do the ward. No kitty litter this time. This was more spell than potion. As such, very little was actually needed, other than sheer magical power.

I guessed that when Lily and the Minehearts had done this on her house, there had been a trinity of them. Trinities were powerful in and of themselves. Add in a Light Witch and well, the magic kind of goes off the charts.

What took them three days? Took us less than three hours. But by the end of it, I was exhausted. That power mostly came from me and using that kind of power can really drain a person.

Maybe I should do this kind of thing as a full-time job. I couldn't really get in trouble with my magic if I kept it depleted on a regular basis, now could I?

But then again, it was me we were talking about.

I'd probably find a way.

Chapter 4

It was a good thing our postman ran early out here in the country. I don't think I could have taken any longer of a wait. As it was, I was standing at the window with my binoculars, watching the mailbox for his arrival. The insurance company had promised the check would be here today.

I was already dressed and prepared for a fun day of car shopping. My plan was to hit the bank and then scope out the local car lots. If I had to, I would even rent an Uber to go a little further afield. I hoped that didn't happen. It's not like I would be all that picky. If it had four wheels and ran, I was pretty much good with it.

Good looks would be a nice extra, but not much of a requirement with me.

When Ruby walked in with her yoga mat, I groaned.

"Not today, Ruby. You know the check is coming today, right?"

She nodded but didn't look very swayed from her original path. Ruby took responsibility very seriously. Mom had entrusted her with my meditation training, and from the looks of things, that was going to happen. Whether or not I wanted it to. Unless...

"Want to go car shopping with me?" It was worth a shot.

Ruby grinned at me. "I'd love to."

Yes!

"Just as soon as we finish up with our meditation. I'm pretty sure the car lots won't sell out in the next few hours."

Ah, well. But I still had one tarot card up my sleeve. "What if I throw in a set of keys so that you can use the car when I'm not? We could totally share it."

It was a bribe, and we both knew it. The only question was, would it work? I saw the wavering of purpose in her eyes. Following her own game of not talking first, I waited.

It was worth the wait.

"Well," Ruby drawled out slowly. "I guess there isn't anything in the meditation rule book that says it has to happen in the morning. As long as you agree to spend some time with me and the mats this afternoon, I guess I'm with postponing it."

If my head hadn't been so firmly attached to my neck, it might have come off with all the enthusiastic nodding I was doing. "You bet!" Then I was looking back out the window again, bouncing on my heels.

"I'm going to go change. Give a shout when he gets here, okay?"

I nodded, and I assumed that Ruby left for her own apartment across the hall. It wasn't like I could hear her leave with that dang quiet shoes spell. I loved it when people couldn't hear me coming, but it was a different story when people used it against me.

This morning, of all mornings, the postman was running late. Ruby was back with me at the window before his plain brown Jeep pulled up beside the box. Within seconds, we were grabbing our backpacks and running down the stairs.

This would be fun.

We almost ran over Aunt Opal on the way to the mailbox. She usually took the stroll down to get it. I briefly saw her raised eyebrows as we raced past. That might have been because we'd almost stampeded her on our way, or it could have been because she'd assumed we were upstairs doing the whole meditation thing.

Either way, it really didn't matter. We got to the box first, and Ruby looked over at me, jerking her head toward the box.

"Go on."

I held my breath and reached out to pull the little metal door open. I didn't start breathing again until I saw the envelope with the Insurance Company's logo and the obvious check inside. Now we were both bouncing on our heels.

Come on, give us a break. We were going to go car shopping. As this was our very first time to do so, it was a big thing to us. Especially to me. I knew the new one won't be as nice as my old one, but I could live with that.

Opal strolled up to us and looked in the box, taking out the rest of the mail. "I take it you got the check, huh?"

I nodded even as I was ripping open the envelope. Everything was just the way the company had promised.

"Yup." Then I thought about it and swallowed. Ruby and I had a couple of different choices. We could get our bikes out and ride into town. However, that would leave us with our bikes in town and no way to get them home. That wouldn't be good.

Or we could take a deep breath and follow through on our second, even less appealing option. I took the deep breath, but come to find out, it wasn't even needed.

"I'm getting ready to go into town myself if you girls want a ride."

You could have knocked me down with a feather. Opal knew we needed a ride... and she wasn't going to make us beg for it? Wow. She really was changing. I think I liked the newer, kinder version.

"That would be great, Opal. Thanks."

She shrugged. "No big deal. I need to check on the store and make sure everything is all right there. Plus, I have a delivery coming today, and I want to pick up some supplies for our spelling session this afternoon." Opal looked into my eyes. "Three o'clock sharp. Don't forget in all your excitement about getting another car."

Opal looked at Ruby and looked like she was going to say something, but she didn't. Most likely, from Ruby's blush, the look was all she needed to convey her thoughts that we were shirking our morning meditation duties. But hey, I'd already promised to make it up later, so I wasn't about to feel guilty about it.

* * *

There were three used car lots within walking distance of the center of Wind's Crossing. The first one we visited had nothing that looked like it would last for any length of time. I wanted something I could get into and drive wherever I wanted to go without the worry of being broken down at the side of the road. The cars there didn't give me any assurance that would be the case.

The second one had real beauties of cars. Unfortunately, they had the prices to match. The salesman assured me that we could work something out, and then he mentioned that they did buy here slash pay here deals, so that if my credit wasn't the best, it wouldn't matter.

It was tempting, especially when I saw a late model Challenger on the lot. But the last thing I needed right now was a car payment. If I couldn't find something that would work for me in town, I could always ask Opie to take me to the city on his next day off. I was pretty certain that the selection would be larger there.

Then I stepped onto the last lot and Betsy caught my eye. Don't ask me why she looked like a Betsy to me, but she did. It was love at first sight. Best of all, the price on the windshield had me doing a double take. In a good way.

When the salesman saw our interest in the little purple convertible doodlebug, he came rushing over, all smiles.

Ruby looked him dead in the eyes. "What's wrong with it?"

His smile faltered for a microsecond, then came back with extra wattage. "Not a thing, really. She's a 2013 model, and the convertible top works great." He motioned up to the now sunny sky. "But with weather like this, who would want to close her up? Am I right? Of course, I am. Just imagine taking this baby for a long drive out in the country with the wind in your hair. Sounds like heaven, don't it? And don't even worry about the price of gas. This girl gets about 40 miles to the gallon on the highway."

Before I could ask where to sign, Ruby stepped in front of me. "I'll ask again. What's wrong with it? That price isn't the price of a car without problems. Not when it looks that nice."

He swallowed, causing his Adam's apple to do a bit of a dance in his throat. She was right. He was holding something back.

I ran my hand over Betsy's hood. Hopefully, it would be something small that I could get fixed. I started looking the car over, not saying a word. I'd never hear the end of it if I talked first. Not when Ruby was in negotiation mode.

I'd made it to the back of the car when I caught the first whiff of the odor. The salesman, who had been watching me like a hawk, must have seen my nose wrinkle. It was a pretty potent smell.

"Okay," he said, glancing over his shoulder. "You got me. The guy that traded this in hit a skunk and rather than take the time to get the car fumigated, he just switched up to a new model."

Ruby frowned at him. "And you guys didn't think to have that done before trying to sell it?"

The Adam's apple was bobbing again. I was starting to wish that we'd brought a little of Ruby's magical truth spell with us. The witches' council frowned on its use without permission, but times like these, it might have been worth the risk. How likely was the council ever to find out?

"We had the car washed and detailed, but the smell..." he gave a little unconvincing laugh. "Well, it's being persistent, that's all. I'm sure it will wear off in time." He leaned in and lowered his voice. "And truthfully, if this baby didn't have that smell, you'd have to add another few thousand to that price tag. It could work in your favor. Buy the car, give it a really good cleaning, not the quick once-over the detail shop gives them, and she'll be right as rain. And you'll have saved a wad of cash."

Ruby didn't look so sure, but I was pretty much sold.

"Has it been checked out by a mechanic?"

He nodded. "Sure has. Got a clean bill of health, too." Another glance over his shoulder. "I'm really not supposed to do this, but if you buy this car today, I'll even throw in a two-year warranty against anything major that could possibly go wrong with her. You won't find a better deal anywhere else; I promise you."

Well, I certainly wouldn't find a better deal in Wind's Crossing. That much was sure. I was biting my tongue to keep from jumping on it, but I wanted Ruby's okay first.

She walked slowly around the car, fingering every little dent and scratch, there were a grand total of three—all of them minor. When she got to the trunk, she motioned for me to pop it and I did. The smell got a lot stronger.

I was kind of glad I was at the front of the car.

"Goddess!" Ruby said, backing away. "Did something die in there?"

If so, then whoever owned the car must not have found it right away. This was more than a simple skunk incident.

She slammed the trunk lid back down and made her way back to me. "I don't think so, Amie. That is one bad smell."

I agreed about the smell, but I really thought with a good cleaning, I could help that. And the car itself had to be a good one or no way would he have offered a two-year warranty.

After a pointed stare, the salesman took the hint and walked a few steps away to give us room to talk privately.

"What do you really think, Ruby?" I mean, it could have been an act for the salesman's benefit. Ruby was an ace negotiator.

"Truthfully, I think you should keep looking." She glanced over at the guy leaning on the hood of another vehicle. He looked particularly shady. And anxious. Like this sell meant more to him than he was letting on. "I don't trust him. Why would they lose thousands on the sale of a car if all it needed was a good cleaning?"

I'd admit that I thought there was more to the story too, but the truth was, after three car lots this was the only vehicle that even came close to being what I wanted as well as what I could afford. Maybe the smell was a blessing in disguise. Just to let me get into the car for a price I could afford.

Ruby blew out a breath. "You're buying it, aren't you?"

I nodded.

"Okay then, let's do this. But let me do the talking. You know I'm better at this than you are."

I wasn't going to argue. She was right.

She ended up getting the manager to come down another five hundred dollars. It might not be enough to cover the sales tax, but it would help with the title and license fees. That was a nice little added bonus. Plus the warranty.

By noon, I was the proud owner of Betsy. With keys and everything. I handed Ruby the extra set. After all, I'd promised.

She didn't seem too keen on taking them, but she did. I didn't think she would want to borrow Betsy until I got that smell taken care of. Personally, I didn't see the problem. As long as the weather held, I could drive with the top down. That should take care of most of the odor right there.

Who would have thought I'd luck into such a good deal on my very first time of car shopping?

Chapter 5

It would be a few days before I got the paperwork to file for registration at the Bureau of Motor Vehicles, so once the last signature was done and we got the keys, we still had a few hours to kill before the spell lesson deadline.

"Wanna go into the city and do a little shopping?"

Ruby rubbed her nose as we walked over to my new car. "Not really. I kind of just want to go home, actually. I called Mom while you were tied up, and she's still at the shop. I think I'll just walk over there and meet her." Then she lifted her eyes to mine. "But don't think I've forgotten your promise. We'll do the meditation session after supper. And wherever you go, you'd better not be late for Mom. You know how she is about karma spells."

Boy, did I ever. But I'd really hoped she'd learned her lesson after the last fiasco. I should have realized that my family's stubbornness was of a stronger stock than that.

"I'll be there. Promise."

She nodded, waved, and walked off quickly.

I was starting to get offended. It wasn't like Ruby to turn down a trip into the city for shopping.

There wasn't too much time to ponder, though, because that's when my cell phone went off. Mabel.

"Hey, girl," I said. "You at the library? I've got something to show you."

"Not now, Amie. I'm in trouble. Can you come to the library? Like right now?"

And just like that, my day dimmed a bit.

"On my way."

I hopped into the car and started her up. The smell was a bit stronger when you were actually sitting in it, but there would be time to worry about that later. Right this minute, Mabel was taking up my worrying capacity.

What had Ralph done now?

Mere seconds later—small town—I pulled up outside the library and parked. A glance at the library doors showed the closed sign was still hanging on them. No sign of lights inside, either.

That was odd.

I climbed out of Betsy and started toward the building. That's when I heard the voices. They were coming from the public parking lot behind the building.

As soon as I rounded the corner, I saw the problem. No questions required for that. What with Ralph's body lying motionless on the ground in a large pool of blood, it was more than obvious.

Mabel and Tommy were both there, standing about ten feet away from the body and looking very guilty. What had they done?

She looked up and saw me, and I could tell she'd been crying. "Amie, what do we do?"

I took a deep breath and walked over to them. From there, I had a closer look at the body. No question he was dead. No need to call for the paramedics, but the sheriff might not be a bad call to make. In fact, I was kind of wondering why they'd called me and not him.

"What happened?"

Tommy started to speak, but Mabel laid her hand on his arm and shook her head.

"I killed him," she said. When Tommy started to speak again, she rushed on. "I think it might be considered self-defense, but I'm not sure. He came into the library last night right before closing time, more than a little drunk. After I closed up, he wanted to… you know, right there at the circulation desk. When I said no, he started in on me." She shivered. "Always before I've just taken his beatings, but last night something just snapped. There was a piece of wood behind the counter from the last repair job, and I grabbed it and hit him with all my might."

I frowned, still looking at the body lying right out in the open beside his car. If she'd killed him in the library, which I wasn't at all sure I believed, how did his body get out here?

"When he went down, I ran," she said. "And I didn't go home last night, either. I really didn't know I'd killed him. I swear it."

"That's because you didn't kill him," Tommy said. "That's what I've been trying to tell you. I'm not going to let you take the blame for something I did." He looked over at me. His face was so set that it could have been carved in stone. "I was here last night, waiting by the back doors."

He glanced over at Mabel. "I'd heard that Ralph had been drinking heavily that afternoon, and I was hoping to convince her not to go home to him. She came out so fast, she didn't even see me. Or lock the back door, which is totally unlike her. I didn't know what to do. After she left, I started to go into the library to see if I could tell what happened, but Ralph came out.

To say he was angry doesn't even begin to cut it. He saw me and he must have put two and two together, because he took a swing at me."

Then he went quiet. Both of them were looking at me. As if I could fix this.

Even a Light Witch can't fix dead.

"Let me take a stab at this. You two fought and when he went down, you left too. Didn't know he was dead?" I was leading him with my question. I knew that wasn't a good interrogation technique, but these two were my friends. Good friends.

"Exactly. I went home and found Mabel at my door crying. We… we went to a motel out of town. Nothing happened, but I didn't want Ralph waking up and then coming to find her and cause trouble." He locked gazes with me. "As mad as he was when he saw me, I think he would have killed her."

"Okay, I think I've got the picture. We need to call the sheriff." Personally, at this point, I wasn't at all sure that either one of them had killed Ralph. Neither of them had mentioned a gun or a knife, and there was an awful lot of blood on the ground under and around the body for just a simple fight.

Mabel just stared at me. "That's it? That's your advice? Call the sheriff?"

What had she been expecting my advice to be? Don't worry I'll help hide the body? I had too many things I was hiding from the world right now to add more.

"Sheriff Taylor is a good man. We can't keep this from him. I take it you found him like this when you came to open the library?"

They both nodded. Then they started arguing again between the two of them over who had killed him and what to tell the sheriff.

Looked like it was up to me to make that call.

* * *

The sheriff's car pulled to the curb a scant two minutes after my call. Opie's personal car closely followed it. No squad car for desk jockeys. Even temporary ones.

I nodded to the sheriff. "I thought he was still on strict desk duty."

Sheriff Taylor grunted. "Yeah, when you're involved, try telling him that."

"The two of you can see me standing here, right?"

I smiled at him. "I just don't want you to get in trouble with the boss man." Fat chance since that happened to be his dad. Still, I didn't want him to get in trouble with any other powers that be either. With all that being said, I was glad he was there. He was friends with Mabel and Tommy too. Maybe he could talk some sense into them.

It dawned on me that the sheriff was just staring at me. When he saw he had my attention, he said, "A little more information than 'hightail it to the library' might be nice."

What could I say? I thought about it for a minute and then just gave up. "Follow me. It's pretty self-explanatory."

We turned the corner to the tiny employee parking lot and Tommy and Mabel jerked apart. She'd been leaning on him pretty heavily. They needed to get a grip on that side of things until this got squared away. They wouldn't want the whole town thinking maybe this wasn't Ralph's fault after all. Funny how men were expected to fool around a little on the side, but the wives were supposed to hold true to their vows. It wasn't fair, but that seemed to be how small towns like ours worked all the same.

The sheriff nodded to the two of them, then walked over and took a closer look at the body. When Mabel started to say something, he just held up a hand to stop her. After going all the way around the body, he looked over at me.

"You take any pictures yet?"

I shook my head. The thought hadn't even crossed my mind. "All I've got with me is my cell phone. Would that work?"

"Better than nothing." He glanced around. "Get everything you can, but stay back as far as you can too."

While I started snapping photos with my cell, he headed over to Mabel. "Looks like he's been dead for a while. Want to explain why I'm just now getting a call?"

I'd been halfway afraid they would change their story from the time they had talked to me, but luckily, they didn't. The sheriff heard them both out in silence. He was good at taking things in without having to interrupt their flow. A person could get a lot of information that way.

Once they both wound down, each one of them still claiming guilt for Ralph's death, he finally spoke.

"Tommy, you say he walked out of the library on his own, right?"

"That's right, so Mabel's in the clear, isn't she? She didn't kill him, I did."

"But…" Mabel started to protest, but the sheriff held up his hand again.

"I'll get to you in a minute. Right now, I'm talking to Tommy."

She didn't look happy, but she kept her mouth shut.

"So, you said he walked out, saw you and got angry. Then he took a swing at you and the two of you fought. Is that accurate?"

"Yes, sir. I didn't mean to kill him. I really thought I just knocked him out. Once he was down, I left." He stole a glance over at Mabel. "I was more worried about her at the time."

Sheriff Taylor nodded. "I can understand that." He paused, looking back to the body. "This next question is extremely important, and I want you to be sure before you answer it. Did either of you draw a weapon? A knife or a gun?"

Tommy actually started, his eyes widening. "Absolutely not!"

"All right then. I'll need the two of you to go to the station with Opie and give formal statements to him. I'll get a scene crew out here and start collecting evidence, if any survived the night."

"But it's me you'll be arresting, right?" Tommy wanted that settled right away.

"Right now, I'm not arresting anybody. But I want your statements, and I don't want either of you taking any trips out of town. Got it?" They nodded. "Good. Now call Clarence and tell him the library will be closed today. It can reopen tomorrow, but we don't need to give people an excuse to be hanging around here."

"I already called him. He wasn't happy, but he understood."

Opie herded them up the alley, then turned back to me. "You okay?"

"Yeah. I only got a few minutes lead on you guys." I gave him a sad smile. "Take good care of them, okay?"

"Kid gloves, I promise." Not that I would expect anything else from him. My fellow was a good guy all the way around.

Once they were gone, I looked at the sheriff. "There's a whole lot more blood than I'd expect from a person who was beaten to death."

"Yup, my thoughts too." He rubbed his chin with his thumb.

"I'm really wanting a look at the front of him. But I don't want to move him until the team processes the scene. Don't want to mess this one up. I like those two, and as much as I probably shouldn't say this, Ralph had been asking for something like this to happen to him for quite some time. People around here like Mabel and they knew how things were between them. Even if she never said a word against the man. They knew."

It made me feel a lot better knowing that the sheriff wasn't going to rush on with arresting Tommy. I'd figured Mabel would be in the clear. But Tommy's confession had a little more meat to it. As far as we knew no one had seen Ralph alive after Tommy left him lying there.

That didn't look good for him.

"I do have one more question for you," he said, not looking me in the eyes. "Would you mind very much telling me what the hell that smell is?"

Chapter 6

Time passes quickly at a crime scene.

For now, I was content with letting the actual law enforcement authorities handle the murder investigation. Sheriff Taylor and I seemed to be on the same page, and neither of my friends had been arrested. So far, so good.

Besides, I had a promise to keep. As I may have mentioned, promises mean a bit something extra for witches. We don't take them lightly. If a witch gives you her word, you can count on it. As long as the witch is worth her salt, anyway. I was.

If I had thought the smell would have dissipated a bit from the car while I was doing my thing at the back of the library, I would have been mistaken. I didn't however, expect for the smell to actually grow worse.

It had.

Before, it took me being within reach of the car to notice it. This time it hit me as I turned the corner from the alley onto the street out front. I was thinking perhaps Ruby had been right about waiting.

Then again, I come from the most powerful family of air witches I know of. Not to mention the fact that I'm now an uber-powerful Light Witch. Surely, we could find a way to deal with the odor emanating from the car.

If the Goddess were truly on my side, maybe I could even talk Aunt Opal into that being the focus spell for today's lesson. I wasn't too hopeful about that though. Most spells took a bit of preparation. Likely an odor-reducing spell or potion would need special ingredients. But there was always tomorrow. And just maybe, if Opal could point me in the right direction to find the spell, I could even try it solo.

Experience had to be a good thing, right?

As per my usual, I walked through the front door just a few minutes to three. Right on time.

Opal's eyes lit up when she saw me. I still wasn't used to that. She was really enjoying these spell and potion sessions. I guess having that little extra oomph was making it fun for her. I didn't mind that one bit. A happy Opal was much easier to be around, especially in a learning capacity.

She took one step toward me before her eyes widened and her smile vanished. "What the hell is that smell?"

I hadn't wanted to admit to myself that the smell had attached itself to me when the sheriff had mentioned it. With Opal mentioning it too, I had to consider the fact that I might be in denial.

Lifting one arm I took an exploratory sniff. Yup. There it was. Fainter than in the actual car, but then that wasn't saying a whole lot.

Opal pointed up the stairs. "Shower first." She paused. "You still have some of that peppermint soap of yours?"

I nodded.

"Use it. A lot of it. Just don't dawdle."

Taking her suggestion, I headed up for a short shower. Then I took another, longer one. At this point, I was partly convinced that the smell was simply ingrained in my brain. No way it had survived two showers with an abundance of peppermint soap.

At least my brain had toned it down a bit. When I figured it was as good as it would get, I went down to Opal.

Her sniff and wrinkled nose told me that just maybe the smell wasn't all in my head after all. But at least now it had to compete with the good smell of peppermint. That helped.

She looked me in the eyes. "Ruby wasn't lying about that car, was she? You bought it when it smells like this?"

All I could do was shrug. I couldn't exactly say I hadn't, could I?

"I kind of figured if soap, water, and air fresheners didn't deal with it, we could try a spell. You don't happen to have one handy we could do for the lesson today, do you?"

That got a bark of a laugh. "Nice try. Maybe tomorrow if the cleaning thing doesn't work." She sniffed again. "I'll start gathering the ingredients in the morning."

The spell she had in mind for today's lesson was usually considered to be a simple one which kind of surprised me. I'd thought with my new abilities, she would be reaching for the harder, more complicated spells. Then I realized that what she was going for today wasn't difficulty of spell, but its range of field.

We were doing a cleansing spell. Normally, you had to prepare a separate spell for each room of the house. With an old farmhouse like ours, with four individual living spaces in it, there would be a lot of time required to get to everything. According to Opal, we were shooting for the whole thing at once.

It would be tricky because it would require that we moved around the house while invoking it.

I looked down at the large pile of dried ingredients that we were about to light on fire. "Is there enough?"

Dried things burnt pretty quickly, and there was a lot of house to cover.

Opal grinned and held up a large plastic baggy with more. "I think I've got us covered."

Good thinking to bring along backups.

"So, let me get this straight. We just repeat the chant in each area we're in while we move the burning incense from room to room, right?"

She nodded. "That's it in a nutshell. A simple spell to put together. Even a full-on non-magical human can do one of these." Opal smiled at me. "But it wouldn't have that oomph that this one will have. With all the goings on this house has seen in the last few weeks, and with everyone's tensions running on high speed, this should help clear the air around here a bit."

I was all for that. Things had been a bit tense here in the farmhouse for a while now. If this would help ease that, I was game.

Putting the ingredients together hadn't taken all that long. The spell's delivery and invocation did. It was kind of cool, though, watching my magic work. Feeling my hair float around me and the magic flow through me—I didn't think I'd ever tire of that feeling. As long as it was controlled, like this was, it was nice. Really nice.

When we were done, I headed up for yet another shower. The incense was a nice smell, don't get me wrong. But for some reason, it was clashing heavily with the used car smell. The combination odor wasn't pleasant in the slightest.

Besides, a shower would be my own cleansing spell. I'd need it before meeting Ruby for our meditation session.

At least this time, I'd have my chair. If I could just stay awake this time, I'd be okay.

* * *

We'd had a late lunch, so it would be a late supper meal too. Opal had volunteered to make it without our help. As I said, she'd been changing into a more approachable person lately. It was freaking me out just a bit, but that didn't mean I didn't like it. Especially if it kept me from having to peel potatoes.

The bean bag chairs where a tad on the heavy side, but we managed to get them out and down the outside stairs, anyway. Ruby had been insistent. She wanted to test out her theory that being outside would put us firmly in the Goddess' view. I had to admit that it felt kind of nice, sitting in the meditation position on my soft comfortable chair with the breeze caressing my face and hair. I could almost imagine that it was the Goddess touching me.

In a way, it was, when you really thought about it.

I'd been expecting it to take a while for me to reach my inner sanctuary. It always had before. Not this time. I closed my eyes, took my ten deep breaths, counting backward, and there it was right before me.

There was something odd, though. It wasn't empty like it normally was. Sure, I knew that you could summon someone—living or dead—to give you advice inside your private happy place. But I was pretty sure I hadn't done that.

So why was this beautiful woman waiting for me?

And she was beautiful. Breathtakingly so. I'd always thought Ruby was the most beautiful woman I'd ever seen. Now, she was a firm number two. But then again, as I got closer, I realized that there was no way anyone could ever compete with Her.

I fell to one knee, my head bowed.

Laughter as soft and melodious as a breeze through wind chimes drifted over me. All my troubles and worries vanished for just that instant, replaced with awe and wonder. For the first time in my entire life, I was truly at peace.

"There's no need for that, child. Rise. I need to speak with you for a bit."

Slowly, I lifted my head. I was almost afraid to move. Afraid that she'd disappear.

"Meow." I turned my head to see my little calico kitten, Destiny, walking up to me. Then I realized that the "Meow" hadn't been in kitten talk, but human. Could cats talk while in my sanctuary? That would be so cool.

The laughter wafted by. "Cats can do whatever you'd like them to here, child." The Goddess motioned around her. "Here you are the master. Anything can happen, but only if you allow it to."

I wasn't about to mention that I hadn't exactly invited her in. That was a moot point. The Goddess was always welcome in a witches' home. It didn't matter if that was a brick and wood home in the real world or a mental sanctuary. The Goddess was always welcome and present. Just not normally in a physical form that you could actually see.

"Please child, sit." Another bean bag chair appeared beside the solitary one that I'd placed inside my mental getaway, and we both took our seats.

She ran a hand over the soft fur and shook her head. "I'll never understand why these went out of fashion. I do love them, you know."

Hey, I had something in common with the Goddess. How

cool was that?

Destiny jumped up into my lap and raised her tiny little front paws up onto my stomach, trying to get my attention. I was feeling kind of guilty because I hadn't seen her in a week. She was still with her mother and sisters at Lily's. I'd been waiting for the word that she was fully weaned and ready to come home. Maybe that time had come.

"Say something, silly." That was Destiny talking. It took her words for me to realize that I had yet to speak a single word. But what on earth do you say to the Goddess of all?

"Thank you for gracing my sanctuary, Goddess." There, I'd said something. It wasn't much, but it seemed to satisfy Destiny, who promptly curled up in a ball on my lap and rolled over for a belly rub. I wasn't sure if it was the Goddess's influence or just the way things worked here, but I could actually feel the soft and silky fur under my fingers. This was as real as if we'd been sitting in my living room back in the farmhouse.

"No thanks are necessary. My visit, however, was. Necessary that is. It's important that you know a few things."

That would be really nice. I had a lot of questions for her, starting with the whole Light Witch thing.

"Ah yes, I rather imagined that's where you would want to start things off. So be it."

She gave me a beautiful smile, then drew her feet up onto the chair with her. I noticed she was barefoot, just like me. Another thing we had in common. Why wear shoes when you didn't have to?

Of course, our similarity in mode of dress ended there. I was still in my yoga pants and T-shirt. She, on the other hand, was in a long and flowing almost see-through gown. Think white, ultra-expensive lingerie and you'd be on the right track.

Truthfully, I was just thankful that she'd deigned to appear with clothes at all. Seeing her in all her glory might have been too much on my poor heart.

And, yes, that's the point when I remembered that she could read my thoughts as well as hear my words. The heat started climbing into my cheeks.

Her laughter graced us again. "Now I remember why I do so love all you Ravenswinds so much. You are all just too precious to me for words." Then she settled back in the chair and the laughter vanished. "I will want a longer visit later, but for now, there are important issues to warn you about."

Warn me about? I didn't like the sound of that at all.

"I don't particularly like it either, child. But that's the way of nature. We must take the good with the bad." Her face grew solemn. "Take the witches' council, for instance."

If she hadn't had my total attention before, she had it now.

"They are so very full of themselves and not at all what I imagined them to be when I created the organization. They need to get back on track and fast. Things are about to change in your world, and they need to be ready." She locked her eyes on mine, and there was a touch of sadness there. "I'm sorry to have dealt this responsibility to you, child, but it was needed." Her smile was back, but definitely not the lighthearted one from before. "You were needed."

"But I don't even know what I'm doing! Maybe if I'd had access to the magic growing up, I could have prepared a bit more for whatever it is you have planned for me, but now... I really hope you aren't counting on me in a big way. I'm not good at this."

She took a deep breath. "Think about it, child. What would a toddler have done with your kind of power? A teenager? With all those raging hormones?" She shook her head. "I gave you access to your power when the time was right and not a second before. Yes, you have catchup to do, but you're coming along quite nicely, by the way."

I'm glad someone thought so. Maybe she could have a talk with Aunt Opal and Mom for me.

"I'd love to say that you'd have all the time you need to gather yourself and prepare, but that doesn't appear to be the case. Things are moving much faster than I'd at first anticipated. I apologize for that."

"What things?"

She thought for a moment, then shook her head. "You aren't quite ready to know that yet. All I can give you for now is a general warning. Change is coming, and you need to take your aunt's lessons very seriously." She paused for a second. "And it might not hurt to ask your mother for a few lessons in the art of healing. That could come in very handy in the future."

Crapsnackles. If healing would be needed, that meant the change would not be one for the better.

And I was going to be the front line of it. Oh, goody.

The Goddess reached out to touch the tip of Destiny's nose. "You won't be alone on the front line, dear. You have your family, the strongest witches I've ever known. And you have Destiny here. She's a bit special. You see, she was conceived while her mother was still Arc's familiar. That took a bit of doing, mind you, but I pulled it off. Now, there's a little piece of me in each of the kittens."

I had to push past the lump in my throat. "Is that why she can talk to me?"

The good smile was back, and she nodded. "Yes. Although, it isn't actually talking you know. It's more like... sending you messages directly to the in-box of your brain. No one else will hear her, ever, so don't go answering her with people around, or..."

People will think I'm crazy. She didn't have to spell it out. People already thought I was a bit odd; it wouldn't take much for them to think I'd crossed the line into insanity. Having a conversation with my new familiar would probably do that.

"And she can only do that if you allow it," the Goddess continued. "If it makes you too uncomfortable, then simply block your mind to the incoming." She grew pensive. "But I do hope you'll at least consider letting her thoughts in. I think you will need the help she can give you."

I thought about it. "Is it okay if I give myself a little time first to get used to the whole idea?"

She smiled. "Of course, child."

Then it hit me. We'd promised one of the kittens to Patricia Bluespring. And she was a council member.

The Goddess just looked at me. "And you think that was by accident, do you? Patricia will be another on the front lines. Don't discount her help. You will need it." She hesitated. "She's hiding a pretty big secret, by the way. I fully expect you and your family to stand behind her once it is revealed."

"Yes, Goddess." Patricia wasn't my most favorite of people, but if the Goddess said I would need her help, then I'd give her all the support I could.

"Good. It's time to put the past behind us and prepare for the future. I'm glad you can see that." She tilted her head as if listening to voices in the distance, which I guess she was.

"Our time is drawing to a close, I'm afraid. But I want to tell you one more thing. I have a message for Ruby and Arc. They are worried that if they become a couple and mix their bloodlines, their offspring will be Light Witches. You need to tell them that won't happen. Their children will be divided between the elements. Girls for Air, and Boys for Earth." She shrugged. "That seems fair to me."

I could feel my mouth drop open. "Ruby and Arc are going to have kids?"

Her smile only grew in brilliance, and she winked at me. Right before reaching out to touch my forehead.

I opened my eyes to find Ruby and Opal's concerned faces staring down at me.

I was back.

Chapter 7

"You were glowing!" Ruby's eyes were wide as she stared down at me.

A quick glance over at Opal showed her eyes were a tad wide too. Whatever they'd seen here on this end couldn't hold a candle to what I'd seen on my end.

"Are you all right, child?" Opal asked. "What happened?"

It was a struggle to get the lump out of my throat, but I finally managed to do it. That freed my voice.

"I met the Goddess."

Opal's eyes closed, and she sank down to sit on the grass beside my chair. "Of course, you did."

It made me feel a bit guilty. From Opal's reaction, I gathered that she'd never found the Goddess in residence at her sanctuary. Personally, I'd have traded places with her on that respect in a heartbeat. I wasn't quite sure how to handle the whole Goddess thing on a much more personal, and physical, level.

"If it helps, she mentioned how much she loves all of us Ravenswinds," I said softly. Then I turned to Ruby. "And she sent a message for you and Arc too." I glanced over at Opal, then mouthed. "Tell you later."

No need to cause added stress to Opal. At the moment she seemed like my news was enough to cause her anxiety meter to raise to the danger zone.

"I take it she explained some things to you?" Opal asked. "It might be nice if you'd share that with us too. I know this whole Light Witch thing affects you most of all, but it would be really helpful to know just what the heck she was thinking when she granted you that power."

"I'll tell you all about it, but right now, I need a drink. Water would do, but I'd love something with a little more kick." After the conversation I'd just had, the kick might be more than necessary.

We went inside and settled in Mom's empty apartment. I wished she hadn't gone home to Archie quite so soon. I could have used her support.

Ruby ran upstairs and came back down with a chilled bottle of wine. After a few sips, I felt a little more focused and centered. Coming back from the sanctuary had never really required a recovery period before. I was thinking that had more to do with the Goddess than anything.

Then I told them everything. Well, almost everything. I wasn't sure about the whole Destiny talking to me thing, so that part—and the part about her being part of the Goddess, or was that the other way around?—I kept to myself.

But everything else, I spilled. Her disappointment in the witches' council, the change coming, Patricia's big secret about to be revealed, all of it. When I got to the Goddess' personal message to Ruby, I paused, then just blurted it out.

Opal needed to know that whatever was between the two of them, which sounded like a lot more than I'd imagined, had the full blessing of the Goddess. Time to put her personal prejudice against Earth witches aside.

They both looked stunned, but then it might not have been

what I ended with. I mean, any of my news could have gotten that reaction. Right?

"You and Arc?" Opal's voice sounded tight. "Didn't you learn from Sapphire's mistake?"

Mistake? My feathers got a little ruffled on that one. I stepped in before Ruby could utter a word.

"You're saying I'm a mistake? Even after the conversation I just had with the Goddess? She planned this, Opal. If you have any issues with it, you might want to take it up with Her."

Opal ran a hand down her face and shook her head. "You're right. I'm sorry. You aren't a mistake. I just wish…"

That the change didn't have to happen in our generation? Yeah, I was right there with her on that one.

"It's okay, Mom," Ruby said softly. "I didn't mean for it to happen. But I think Arc is my destiny." She smiled over at me. "Funny how that worked out, name wise and all."

She was referencing to the fact that I had named him Destiny back when he'd been a cat. I had thought at the time that he was my destiny. Interesting that instead, he was Ruby's.

"Love doesn't always give us a choice." Opal still didn't sound too happy about it, though. "Give me time, I'll get used to the idea. Just… give me time."

Ruby nodded and then looked over at me. "Anything else you want to tell us?"

Nope. Not a thing.

Opal stood. "All right. We'll deal with this as it comes. Now let's eat before the food gets any colder."

* * *

We'd finished our meal of spaghetti and garlic bread knots

and were just getting ready to call it a night when the car pulled into the drive. A glance outside showed the sheriff climbing out of his vehicle.

Opal had the door opened before he even got onto the porch.

"Good evening, Sheriff," she said. "I hope this is a social call. Though from your vehicle of choice, I'd have to guess that isn't the case. Please tell me Sapphire is all right?"

I held my breath until he nodded. Funny, but that thought hadn't even occurred to me. Trust Opal's thoughts to go there first.

He looked over at me and gave a lopsided smile. "Actually, I'm here to see Amie, if she has a little time to talk. Sorry to come so late, by the way."

Actually, his timing couldn't have been better. A little earlier and who knows what he might have interrupted.

"Sure, Sheriff," I said. "This about Ralph?"

"Yeah." His hand went up to ruffle through his hair. "I think I'm going to need your help on this one. As much as it truly pains me to admit that."

"Ralph?" Opal asked. "Ralph Morgan? Mabel's husband? What about him?" Then her face set into a dangerous expression. "He hasn't hurt Mabel, has he?"

"Kind of the opposite, actually, if you listen to her story." Sheriff Taylor looked at me with a definite question in his eyes.

"I know it's weird I haven't told them yet, but things around here are a little on the crazy side right now."

"That must be true if you forget to tell them you stumbled on a dead body."

"What?" That was both Ruby and Opal. I'd get to them in a minute. Right now, I had to set the sheriff straight.

"I didn't stumble onto Ralph. Mabel called me. They're the

ones that found him." How did he not know that?

"And you didn't think to tell us?" Opal's voice didn't sound happy.

I lifted a shoulder. "I'm sorry. But I was running so close on time, then you sent me up to shower, and then with the spelling and… things… it must have slipped my mind for a while." Turning back to the sheriff, I asked the burning question. "They're both still free of suspicion, right?"

He gave a short laugh. "I wouldn't go so far as to say that, but neither of them has been arrested, if that's what you're asking."

It was, and he knew it.

Opal was standing off to the side with her arms crossed. Obviously, she wasn't happy about being kept out of the informational loop. Not that I had done so intentionally. That wouldn't matter a bit to her. I'd have some serious making up to do after this. Especially as it followed being the first one in the family to go one on one with the Goddess.

"We can talk upstairs if you want."

He looked up the stairs and shook his head. Most likely he remembered the fact that the inside entrance to my apartment went directly into my bedroom. The sheriff was an old-fashioned kind of guy. Even if we did have suspicions that maybe he and Aunt Opal had a little something going on between them.

They hadn't shared that little update with us, so for now mum was still the word.

"I'm thinking maybe the porch would be a better option."

I followed him out, and we both sat on the porch swing. It took a couple of full swings for him to gather his thoughts enough to start.

"We don't have the coroner's final report back yet, obviously, but off the cuff, he feels that Ralph died from two deep stab wounds in his chest and stomach area."

"That's good news, right? I mean, Tommy may have punched him, and Mabel may have hit him over the head, but neither one of them stabbed him. So, we're looking at someone else as the killer then?"

He nodded, but not the nod of a man certain that was the answer.

"Initially, that's the direction I'm taking things. But you should know by now that people lie. Especially when there's a murder being investigated. All we have right now are statements from Tommy and Mabel that say no weapons were involved in either of their attacks."

I thought about it for a minute. Even though I didn't want to admit it, he was right. If I really had killed someone it would be pretty smart of me to confess to doing so… as long as I did so in a manner that would eventually clear me of the crime. But the truth is, I couldn't see either Mabel or Tommy being devious enough to think of that.

"I don't think they lied, sheriff. Mabel was really upset when she called me. Hysterical even. If she'd stabbed him, I think I would have gotten that call last night. I don't think she knew he was dead."

"What about Tommy Hill?"

More thinking. "I'm thinking maybe Tommy and Mabel have a little flirting going on. And I think that Tommy would defend Mabel if it came to it. Maybe even take a murder charge on himself to save her from being sent up for it. But I've never known Tommy to be violent. Or to carry a knife for that matter."

The sheriff grunted. "Yeah, Opie said the same thing. You

two know them better than I do, so I'm willing to take your opinions into serious account."

The swing made a few more rounds in silence. He was the one that was coming to me for help. I was curious as to what that help entailed, but I wasn't going to make it easy on him. I was going to make him ask for it.

Eventually, he did.

"I can't pay you for this. I need to get that right out in the open and upfront. However, I would sure appreciate it if you would have a heart to heart with Mabel and see if you can get her to be totally straight with you about everything. How things were with her and Ralph, who had it in for him, her relationship with Tommy. Everything. Right now, she's so focused on protecting Tommy that I just don't think we're getting the full story."

My heart gave a little twitch. I wasn't at all sure how I felt about what he was asking me to do. I mean, sure I would do it. I'd already planned on it once the initial talking to the police thing panned out. But what I hadn't planned on doing was making a report of my findings to the sheriff once I'd talked with her.

Which I was thinking Sheriff Taylor knew before he came out here. This was just his way of telling me he expected to be kept in the loop.

Dang that witch's promise thing. I had to be very careful about how I worded my next few responses.

"So, what you're asking me to do is rat out my friends if they tell me anything important."

"No, I'm asking you to help me put a killer behind bars. I know Ralph Morgan wasn't the best of men. Personally, I couldn't stand the man. But even the ones like Ralph deserve justice. And once someone kills, well, it's easier to do it again."

I didn't like the sound of that last part.

"I'd already planned on talking with Mabel tomorrow, but I'm guessing you knew that. If I learn anything pertinent to the case that I think will help you put the killer behind bars, I'll tell you."

He just looked at me. "You do know that I would be a better judge of what's pertinent to the case than you would be, don't you?"

All I could do was smile at him. "Then you'll just have to rely on your great interrogation skills to learn those things, won't you?"

Taking a deep breath, he nodded. "All right. We have a deal. Just… keep an open mind and err on the side of caution, okay?"

"Sure thing, sheriff." I paused as he started to stand up. "I'm guessing there's a reason you haven't asked me to talk with Tommy? Is Opie doing that one for you?"

He hesitated before answering the question. "We both thought that would be the best option, all things considered."

Yeah, they were probably right on that one. Tommy Hill and I definitely had a history.

Chapter 8

The next morning, I was up and at 'em super early. Part of that was the fact that I wanted to catch Mabel at home before she left for the library. If she was even going to work that day. Clarence might just be on his own for a few days there. Hopefully, he wouldn't give her too much grief about it. With him, it could go either way. He could be supportive when the times called for it, but then again, he didn't like anything that created extra work for him. I was hoping he'd lean toward the supportive angle on this one.

The other part of my early hour was trying to beat it out of the house before Ruby got up. After the goings-on of yesterday, I wasn't all that eager to go to my sanctuary this morning. In fact, it made me tense just thinking about it.

Meeting the Goddess had been great, don't get me wrong. But the whole change is coming thing was a bit too ominous for my liking. And what was the big secret that Patricia Bluespring was keeping from the world? Would she let it slip? Or was something bad going to happen to reveal it without her help?

There were too many unanswered questions for me to think that I'd be able to sit and meditate for the hour my mom prescribed. So, yeah, I was kinda running away.

I closed the door out onto the second-floor balcony as quietly as I could. Not that it did me any good. Opal was waiting for me at the bottom of the stairs.

She wasn't alone, either. Billy Myers stood there with her, grinning up at me. "Good morning, Ms. Amethyst."

I smiled back at him. Billy's grins were so open and friendly that they were kind of contagious. "Good morning, Billy. What you are out and up to today?"

"Ms. Opal here has asked me to take a look at maybe putting in a gazebo over there for you all. A medication garden, I think she called it."

"That's meditation, Billy, but you got it close," Opal said gently. "It's just a fancy way of saying to sit around and be quiet with your thoughts."

"Ah," he said. "Meditation. I'll have to remember that word. I do that a lot. Good to know there's a name for it."

"We were hoping we could borrow your thoughts on it before you rushed off to see Mabel."

That's the thing about Aunt Opal. She always knew. Even when we didn't want her to. This time, I figured she must have been listening in on me and the sheriff's front porch conversation last night. Most times, I didn't have a clue how she did it. She was just that good. And there was always the possibility that there was a touch of magic involved.

"What do you need my thoughts on?"

Billy hefted up a heavy artist's sketchpad. "I brung some drawings of some really cool outdoor buildings that struck my fancy. All you guys have to decide is if one of them will work for you. I'm pretty sure I can do all of these."

Opal and I sat down on the bottom step to flip through his book. I was impressed.

"Did you draw these, Billy? They're really good."

He blushed. "Thank you, Ms. Amethyst. And yup, I drew all of them. Pencils and papers help calm my brain down some."

We could all use more of that in our lives. But not all of us could do it with what amounted to a real talent. Billy could.

It was on the sixth flip of the page that we stopped. That was the one. Hands down and no question about it.

The structure was a super simple one. No fancy trim work or designs. There was a single step leading up to a plain wooden floor. Four heavy wooden posts, one at each corner of the flooring, supported the simple style of roof that would provide shade and shelter from sun and rain both. The only ornamentation to it was a simple latticework that edged the top of the structure directly under the roof. The absence of walls meant that one could commune fully with the surrounding nature while staying cool and dry at the same time.

Perfect.

Opal looked at me, and when I nodded my agreement, she handed the pad back to Billy. "This is the one we want."

He looked at it and smiled. "Good choice. I really like that one. It just looks… peaceful."

"That's what we're going for all right," Opal agreed. "How long you think it would take to build something like that?"

Billy's face scrunched up for a minute. "I'd say I could have it done in a week or so. Might not even take that long." Then he paused, and the color returned to his cheeks. "I'd have to ask for some of the money upfront though. It's not that I don't trust you, but I'll need to buy the lumber and stuff and get it delivered here too."

"That's not a problem, Billy. If you'd work up a price for me, I'll be happy to pay it all upfront if you need it. You're one of the few people in town that I'd trust that far, but you're an honest man."

He smiled at her. "Thank you, Ms. Opal, that means a lot to me."

I stood up and brushed a wandering leaf off my jeans. "So, if we're done here…"

Opal stood too. "Go on. Do what you need to do. Just be back by three, all right?"

"Not a problem."

"And do me a favor and get that car washed and cleaned before you get back home too. That smell is starting to drift."

Yeah, I'd noticed that too.

* * *

Even with the slight delay, I still managed to get to Mabel's modest-sized house in plenty of time to catch her before she left for the library. One look at her after she opened the door, though, and I knew that time really hadn't been a factor at all. She wasn't going anywhere today. Not for several hours, anyway.

"Did I wake you up?" I asked. Not that I thought that was really a possibility. It didn't look like she'd gotten a wink of sleep since I'd seen her the day before. Her puffy and red eyes told of a recent crying bout too.

Mabel just shook her head and stepped to one side to let me in. One thing about Mabel's house. It was always immaculate. Up until this morning, anyway.

A glance into the kitchen—a point against open floor plans in my mind—showed undone dishes and a dirty stovetop. Around the couch and chair in the living room were wadded up pieces of tissue that had cascaded from the mountain of tissues inside the tiny wastebasket between them. This wasn't normal.

She plopped back down on the sofa, and I took one of the chairs.

"Are you okay?" It was a silly question to ask someone whose husband had just been murdered. Especially when they considered themselves at least partly responsible for their death.

Mabel lifted a shoulder and sniffed. "I don't know, really. I did love him, you know. Back in the beginning at least. Before he changed."

More likely he hadn't changed at all but just had begun to show his true colors. But I kept my mouth shut on that for now.

"Why did you stay with him when he started... hurting you?"

She looked away, not meeting my eyes. "You wouldn't understand. You have your family. I don't. I have nothing." Silent tears started rolling down her cheeks.

"You have me. You have friends. They would have helped you. I know I would have." I'm guessing Tommy would have helped too. The question was, did he help a little too much?

"Maybe, but I didn't want them getting hurt because of me. Ralph said if I left him..."

"He threatened whoever took you in, didn't he?"

She nodded but didn't say anything. Right now, I was thinking it was a very good thing that Ralph Morgan was already dead. I'd hate to end up in jail because of a jerk like him. Or worse, on the council's radar.

I thought about how to change the conversation, but in the end, I just did what I usually do. I just did it.

"Do you know anyone that might have wanted Ralph dead? Was he in any kind of trouble?"

Now her eyes met mine. "What do you mean? We know who killed him. Me and… well, me."

I shook my head. "The sheriff doesn't think so. Not if you two have been telling us the truth. He told me that according to the coroner, Ralph had been stabbed. That's most likely what killed him, not the damage you and Tommy did to him."

Her eyes widened and her lips parted slightly. "Are you serious? You aren't just saying that?"

"I wouldn't get your hopes up on this, Mabel. If what you and Tommy said was true and neither of you used a knife on him, then someone other than the two of you dealt that killing blow."

She stood up and started pacing. "Oh, this is wonderful. I didn't kill him. Tommy didn't kill him. Oh, thank you, Amie!"

Now the tears started up again in earnest, but I think they had changed to tears of relief rather than worry, grief, and guilt.

I gave her time to recover a bit, then prodded her a little. "Do you know who that might have been?"

Taking a deep breath, she reached over for another tissue and wiped her eyes before blowing her nose. The tissue hit the mountain and rolled off to join its predecessors.

"Well, he and Marco—that's his business partner if you can call what they do a business—were at it recently. Marco was accusing him of taking out a big draw on the company's account."

"Did he? Take the draw, I mean."

"He wouldn't admit it, but I think he did. He came home with a bunch of high-priced alcohol that night. I know it cost more than we could have afforded. Ralph didn't like the cheap stuff. Thought it was beneath him or something."

Sounded like the man I was being to see for his true self. A loser in every sense.

"Did Marco threaten him?"

Mabel thought for a minute. "Yeah, but not with violence or anything. He said if the money didn't reappear in the account, he'd take legal actions."

If Ralph was a full partner with access to the company's bank account, I really didn't think there were many legal options that would be left to poor Marco. But it wasn't worth going into that with Mabel. That bit of information may have come from Ralph. The real story might be very different.

"Anyone else you can think of?" With Ralph's reputation, I was betting there would be at least a half dozen good suspects within city limits. I wasn't wrong.

"Well, if he treated her anything like he treated me, which I doubt, then his mistress might make the list. But all I know about her is that she wears expensive smelling perfume."

"Ralph was having an affair? Are you sure?"

She nodded. "Oh yes. There were nights when he'd come home from the club reeking of her perfume and with lipstick in places he'd forgotten to wipe off." She blushed. "Some of those places weren't where it would have been possible to get lipstick with your clothes still on."

"Ah." What more could I say?

It took some doing and a lot of leading questions, but I came away from Mabel's with a list of names to start with. I headed to the library before the sheriff's station, though. They had the closest public copy machine that I knew of, and I wanted a copy of this list before I handed it over to Sheriff Taylor, or his desk jockey and my current beau, Opie.

Right now, it was my full intention to let the sheriff and his

61

company handle this one on their own. But if things started looking iffy for Mabel or Tommy, that would change.

I wasn't going to let either of my friends go down for the murder of a jerk like Ralph Morgan.

Chapter 9

After making the copy and dropping it off at the sheriff's office, my next stop was a mandatory one. The car wash.

As there had been no rain in the forecast, the top had been down on my little bug ever since I'd bought it. Any hope of it helping to air out the smell had been a futile one. If anything, the smell had gotten stronger.

When I raised the top in order to go through the car wash, the odor seemed to magnify tenfold. It was all I could do not to throw up from it. I threw open both doors and climbed out into the open trying to catch a breath of clear, odorless air. That wasn't possible in smelling range of the car which seemed to grow every second.

As soon as the roof was firmly secured, I shut the doors. That helped. A little. I just hoped I had enough quarters.

Twenty dollars in change went pretty quickly as I soaped and scrubbed the outside of the car as hard as I could with multiple layers of lathery suds. Then I rinsed it briefly and repeated the entire process, trying to get as much of the underneath of the car as I could as well. It was hard to say exactly where the odor was coming from. It seemed pretty much everywhere.

When I was done and couldn't put it off any longer, I held

my breath and opened the door long enough to dart inside to push the control to open the roof. Then I high-tailed it out of the car wash bay and waited a good five minutes.

By the time I risked going back in—a necessary risk as by this time there was another car waiting for the bay—I had high hopes of a little improvement. They were dashed pretty quickly.

The inside of the car wasn't as bad as it was with the top up, but it was still bad.

Next stop, the local hardware store to rent an upholstery shampoo machine. It took some major doing to get the machine in the car with the limited trunk space, but with the help of a couple of bungee cords, I got the job done.

I parked closer to the house when I got home as I would need to plug in a long extension cord for power. An outlet in Mom's kitchen was the closest, so I got it hooked up and ready to go.

Then I knocked on Ruby's door. When she answered, I grinned at her.

She rubbed her eyes and looked at me with a frown. "You ready for your lesson already?"

It was pretty obvious that she'd just gotten up for the day. She was really milking this extended vacation from the shop for everything it was worth. Right now, I was feeling pretty good about myself. Normally, I was the sleepy-headed bum of the family. Things were really looking up.

"Nope, but I could use your help."

Her eyes narrowed, and she took half a step toward me before backing up big time. Her hand went to cover her nose and mouth.

"Goddess, it's getting worse. What did you do to make it so angry?"

My smile and good mood were fading pretty quickly. "I washed it. Twice. Now I'm going to shampoo the trunk and the inside."

She shook her head, and the door started closing.

"I'll spring for Carney's Pizza for lunch."

The door paused for about two seconds before it finished closing with a final sounding click.

I was on my own.

* * *

When I'd dropped off the papers at the sheriff's office, I'd found that Opie wasn't there. He'd gone to see his doctor. The hope was that he'd be released for full duty again today. On the off chance that he was done at the doc's and had some free time on his hands, I gave him a ring.

I lucked out, too. His dad had given him the rest of the day off in celebration of his release. Well, he was to have a talk with Tommy friend to friend, so he wasn't totally off duty for the whole day. But he had a couple of hours to spare and offered to help me.

And yes, it was the Carney's pizza that sealed the deal. What can I say? The two of us were made for each other.

It didn't take him long to get there. By the time he arrived, I had the machine plugged in and filled with the cleaning solution properly mixed with water. This had better work. I was running out of options, and I didn't want to live the rest of the car's life hearing Ruby's I told you so's.

He pulled in and parked over by the trees, in the shade. When he got out of his car, he nodded appreciatively.

"Cute wheels," he said. "How much did you go into debt on

her?"

A little pride crept in. "Not a penny. Even had enough left over to cover the registration fee and everything."

Opie didn't look like he believed me until he got a few steps closer.

"What the hell is that?"

Yeah, the car wash had seemed to anger it. It had been bad before. Now it was far worse. I wouldn't have thought that possible, but apparently, the car had other ideas.

He wanted to back out, but I wouldn't let him. He'd offered me two hours of his time, and I used every minute of it. I'd picked up a hand scrubber while I was out too, and once he wet down the trunk, I went to town with it. Within those one hundred and twenty minutes, we covered every square inch of the inside of that vehicle.

And it didn't do an ounce of good.

We sat on the bottom step of our outside stairway and stared at the car. It just shouldn't be possible for a single thing to stink so very bad. Especially after all that soap and water.

"Do I still get my Carney's pizza?"

I nodded. It wasn't his fault our efforts had been wasted. Besides, I'd worked up quite a sweat in the last few hours. Funny, but right now I welcomed the slight body odor. It beat the car's smell by a landslide.

We took separate showers as we waited for the pizza. The single showers were necessary as we weren't yet to that point in our relationship where we were having sexual relations. Hey, we were taking it slow, dang it! Mostly because of the whole Light Witch power control thing, but still… slow.

Of course, Ruby was watching for the delivery man, too, and snuck over for a slice. After a moment's internal debate, I let

66

her have one. One. The rest Opie and I had earned doing the work. She should have helped while she'd had the chance.

As we munched, she looked thoughtful. "You know, I've been thinking about that smell your car…" She sniffed. "Okay, and you too, have."

Hadn't we all? It was kind of hard not to think of it what with being surrounded by the stench and all. But she wasn't done.

"I'm thinking it isn't a natural odor. What if your car has been hexed? Maybe by a karma spell or something. The owner might have given up on it and traded it in for a less-smelly version. And you got stuck with the curse that should be on him."

I paused mid-bite. She made a very good point. That would also explain the odor worsening every time we tried to do something about it. Karma spells did that sometimes. Especially if the witch in question had included that little bit into the spell work.

"Is there any way to know who cast it?" I was really hoping she'd say yes. Surely, we could get the witch to reverse it if we could find them.

She chewed thoughtfully, eyeing the remaining pizza. There were two slices left. "I'm not sure. Hunger makes it hard to think."

That got an eye roll from me. And another piece of pizza. I was glad I went with the extra-large. Not that there had been any debate on that. Opie and I could really put Carney's away.

Ruby grinned as she bit into it. "Thanks," she said belatedly around her mouth full of pizza goodness.

She's beautiful as a witch can be, but she isn't all that big on manners sometimes. At least not around friends.

67

"So…" I said.

The grin got bigger as she swallowed the bite. "Oh, I have no way of telling, but Mom might. I know the council has a way of checking magical signatures and stuff. And now that I think of it, there should be a spell mark, shouldn't there? If we could find that, that should tell Mom all she needs to know."

We hurried up and finished the pizza then ran down to the car.

"We should have brought clothespins for our noses," Opie said. You'd think he was joking. He wasn't.

"Just a minute." I ran back upstairs and took three of the cheap face masks out of the pack I'd bought when I went to the animal shelter for my familiar. The one that turned out to be my brother. Boy, was that ever a long story. I sprayed a touch of perfume on the center of the face shields and then hustled back down to the others.

Opie nodded appreciatively. "It isn't perfect, but it will help."

It took us all of five minutes to find it.

A tiny black shape inside a circle. The shape looked oddly like a wolf's head.

I say odd because our spell marks say something about each individual witch. Our family had spell marks that were tiny pentagrams with the color of our gemstone in the very center. I'd actually had a necklace made out of mine. They were tiny but perfect.

So what did a wolf say about the witch that cast it?

And just like that, the dread started seeping in.

Chapter 10

After that, the day passed pretty much as it should have. The spell session with Opal wasn't an odor conquering one after all. According to her, that might make the karma spell extremely angry, and we'd already ticked it off more than we should have. As it was, she made me move my car over to the farthest point of smooth grass away from the house. Now if the breeze would start helping and blow the other way, we'd have it made.

Until I had to go somewhere.

In fact, as it turned out, the spell session didn't really live up to its name at all. Instead, she took the allotted time slot for it to gather us girls together and go foraging. I guessed that was because us finding the spell mark had thrown her off her game, but she wasn't saying that and nothing about her demeanor said it either. She and Mom might be able to read me and Ruby like open books, but the book of Opal was closed up tight.

The woods behind our house was full of all kinds of nifty spell casting ingredients. Some were natural inhabitants and others had been specifically transplanted there by the moms. Either way, they were all thriving. Most of the credit for that went to my mom. She wasn't just a healer for humans. Her powers worked well for plants too.

While we were making our haul, Opal spent the time explaining each plant's name and purpose for spellcraft. So, maybe this was a lesson after all. This was all stuff that I needed to know. As it had been thought I didn't have magic, we'd kind of left this knowledge out of my schooling growing up. Time to change that.

I needed to catch up. And according to the Goddess, I'd better be pretty quick at doing so.

By the time we headed back to make dinner, we each had a good stash of leaves, roots, and fungi in our pouches. Some of it would be dried and used to restock the shop's shelves once Opal decided to reopen. I was betting that wouldn't be too long. Opal wasn't much of one to sit around the house all day doing nothing.

Besides, that shop meant a lot to her. I hated that my current situation was keeping her from it. Yet another, more personal, reason to get this witch with power aspect of my life in order as quickly as possible. So my family could get their normal lives back.

None of us wanted to cook, so we just threw together a quick salad topped with some leftover strips of cooked chicken and cheese. It was cold, but it was good. And with the season finally changing over to summer, a cold meal every now and again was a welcome change.

I took mine to go and headed up to my apartment. I knew I had promised myself—and yes, Opie too—that I'd let the sheriff handle Ralph's death, but it wasn't sitting as well with me as I'd thought it would. I just felt like I wasn't doing right by my friends.

That feeling multiplied when my phone rang, and I recognized Mabel's number.

"Hey, Mabel. You doing okay?"

"Not really, Amie." I could tell that from her voice. There was a definite shake to it. "Last night was really rough here alone…"

Some friend I am. Of course, she shouldn't be alone at night right now.

"Why don't you come and stay with me for a few days? My couch makes a great bed, and it's quiet out here. Maybe that would help your nerves a bit."

There was a brief silence. "You really wouldn't mind?"

"Of course not. I'll even come to get you if you need me to. Though I should warn you, my car has a pretty nasty odor to it. We're trying to fix it, but well, it's fighting us."

"I can drive myself out if you're sure it's okay."

"I am. And if Tommy wants to come over to visit you here, that's fine too."

I heard the breath she blew out even over the phone. Yeah, I'd guessed right. Part of the reason she wanted away from town was so that she and Tommy could talk without getting their neighbors' tongues wagging. Small towns have a reputation for gossip for a reason.

"Thanks, Amie. I've talked with him a couple of times over the phone, but I could sure use him right now. I just wish…"

"No need to finish that sentence, Mabel. I wish you'd found each other before Ralph entered the picture too. It would have been so much better for both of you. You deserve to be happy."

"I never broke my vows you know. To Ralph. I was faithful right up to the end. Even though I knew he wasn't."

Yeah, I needed to work on that angle. There had to be a way to figure out who the mystery woman was. Once we knew, we could add at least one more possible suspect to the list. Two if the woman was married.

The next half hour was a bit of a whirlwind of cleaning. I'm not the best of housekeepers even at the best of times. And the times of late hadn't been the best.

I managed to get the dishes washed and the bathroom semi-clean before I heard steps on the balcony. I opened the door just as Tommy was getting ready to knock.

He stood there blinking at me in silence.

Well, this was awkward. I'd really thought Mabel would be the first to arrive. I hadn't planned to have to handle alone time with Tommy.

"Thank you for letting us meet here," he finally said. "I've been kind of dying a little knowing how bad she's hurting right now and not being able to be with her."

"Hey, it's no problem. She's going to be staying here a few days, I think. Until things settle down a bit. You're welcome here any time." Then I looked him square in the eye. "Nothing more than hugs here, though, okay? I don't want to walk in on something… other than that."

His laugh didn't have an ounce of humor in it. "That's all it's ever been between us. And even the hugs are rare."

Well, yeah. She had been a married woman. That wasn't the case now. That was my whole point. I didn't think he got it yet.

"Look, Tommy. I know you guys played it cool while Ralph was still… well, alive. All I'm asking is that play it cool for just a little longer. Once the sheriff has the killer all wrapped up and behind bars, then maybe things will change. But you don't want to give the neighbors and people in town reason to think you two did away with him so you could be together."

He nodded. "We know that." He motioned around. "That's

why we're here, after all. We're afraid to much more than say hello in town."

"Good. Stay that way for a while. Give the sheriff time to do his job."

That got an odd look. "You aren't working on this too? I thought you were training to be an investigator."

Right now, I really wished I'd kept that choice more to myself. Unfortunately, by now, the whole town knew my future career path choice.

"I'll look into too, Tommy. But I can't promise anything. The sheriff definitely has more resources than I do. He's your best hope for sorting this out."

He might have said more, but that's when Mabel's car pulled around the corner of the house. She got out, and he ran down the steps to meet her.

They ran into each other's arms just like in the movies. Then, after that instant embrace, they walked into the woods holding hands.

I was glad the people in town hadn't seen that. It would definitely have created that shadow of a doubt as to their innocence.

As much as I hated to admit it, now that shadow was in my mind too.

* * *

I don't know what time Tommy finally left, and I really don't care. They spent most of their time out on the balcony anyway, so I didn't have to worry about interrupting anything if I had to go to the bathroom or something. I appreciated that.

Not that I thought I would interrupt anything. Friends

respect other friends' boundaries. Especially when they are in that friend's home.

Mabel had already left for work the next morning when I got up, but she left me a note telling me thanks and that she'd like to stay a couple more days. That wasn't a problem with me. She needed some time to get used to her new normal before spending her nights alone in a house that she and Ralph had shared.

I knew I would if the situation had been reversed.

Today would be a free day for me. At least this morning was free. I had absolutely nothing planned, and as my car was still an odorous beast, I was fully planning to make the most of a day at home doing absolutely nothing. Not that I thought that would really happen, my life being what it is now, but that was the plan.

I'd barely gotten showered and dressed before I heard the vehicle coming down the drive. A glance out the window showed Lily's van out front. She and Arc climbed out and then Arc reached back in and pulled out a cat carrier.

It would appear Destiny had come home. Immediately the guilt set in. I hadn't been over to see her in a week. Not a good way to treat a new familiar.

Lily's expression when I went downstairs to greet them told me she felt the same way. I felt the heat rising in my cheeks.

She pointed to the cat carrier now sitting on the floor by the door. "Destiny has done nothing but howl and complain for the past two days. Last night was the worst of all." Lily shook her head. "I know I said I wanted to give her more time with her mom and sisters, but I'd say she's ready to be your responsibility now."

I swallowed. Great. It would also appear that I might have

ticked off the Goddess with my inattention of Destiny too. After all, she'd said the kitten was a part of her. I didn't know how that worked exactly, but I knew that Destiny would be one very spoiled kitten. I'd make the last week up to her somehow.

"I'll take good care of her, I promise." I lifted the small kennel and looked inside. Destiny looked back out at me. Yeah, the cat was going to be great at the whole guilt thing. She was every bit as expressive as Arc had been as a cat.

Once my thoughts turned to Arc, I started wondering why he had come too. It didn't take two people to deliver a cat.

He grinned at me and then looked past me and up the stairs. "Is Ruby home?"

Ah, so that explained it. He wasn't here to visit me at all. It was his new romantic interest that he wanted time with.

"She's upstairs." I thought about warning him that she might not be out of bed yet, but why spoil the fun?

Halfway up the stairs, he turned to look at me. "If I want to stay longer than Lily, could you give me a ride back home?"

The nerve of him. Here he was totally ignoring his one and only sister and yet he expected me to run him all the way home when he was done spending time with Ruby? I started to say no way, but then it hit me. He'd be riding in my car. My smelly car.

Not that I wanted to ride in it all the way to Oak Hill and back myself, but it might be worth it if I shared half that trip with Arc. In fact, it was just the little bonus I needed to say yes.

I gave him the sweetest smile I could. "Sure thing."

"Thanks." And he took the rest of the steps two at a time. The jerk.

The door to Opal's apartment opened, and she stepped out. "I thought I heard voices out here."

She wasn't fooling me. She'd have known the instant that van turned into our driveway. It was one of her super powers.

"Hello, Opal, we're just dropping off Amie's new familiar," Lily said.

"I don't suppose you'd have a few minutes to spare me before you head back? I'd love your advice on plants and landscaping for our new meditation garden."

And just like that, the two of them walked out the front door and left me standing there alone in the hallway. I glanced inside the kennel at Destiny. "Looks like we're invisible, girl." I paused. "Or just maybe not invited."

"Meow."

I stared at her. The meow wasn't a cat's meow at all. Just the word. I think my cat had an attitude problem. Weren't we going to be a match made in heaven? Or maybe the other place as far as others might be concerned.

Holding her kennel up at chest height, I pointed to Opal's still open door. "Aunt Opal lives in there." Then I turned and pointed to Mom's open door. "My mom used to live in there, but right now it's kind of open for anyone who wants to crash there. She got married to... well, I don't what technical relationship he is to you. Your mother's old familiar's father, I guess. It gets complicated, doesn't it?"

Destiny seemed to agree with me, so I continued upstairs to give her a tour of our more personal living space. After pointing out Ruby's door, we turned into my bedroom. Keeping up a stream of one-sided conversation, explaining where everything was and where her bathroom facilities were located, we walked through the entire apartment. It didn't take long.

Once back in the sitting room, I checked to make sure my bedroom door was closed, and I opened the kennel door.

Destiny strolled out and rubbed against my ankles. I picked her up for a quick cuddle.

Her fur was longer and ever silkier than the cat form that Arc had used. I could so get used to this. Which was a good thing, because this time, it was a forever thing. Or as close to that as I could possibly make it. I wanted us to be close for a very long time.

After a short kitty to human love session, she started squirming to be let down. When I sat her on the floor, she walked straight for the outside door.

"That leads into the hallway and the outside balcony. You don't need to be going out that door," I explained patiently. "You're just a little kitten, and there are hawks and things out there that could hurt you."

Destiny sat on her haunches and her eyes widened. Anyone who says a cat can't out stare a human is full of bologna. I was the first to look away.

I felt like I'd been firmly put in my place.

By a creature not even six inches tall.

Chapter 11

A t Destiny's insistence, I opened the door into the hallway and then the outside door. She scampered down the steps as if she'd been doing them all her little life. What could I do? I followed her.

Billy was already hard at work on the gazebo, and Opal and Lily were standing off to the side of the area deep in discussion. After a brief tour of the backyard, Destiny made her way straight for Billy.

He was bending over to pick up his hammer, and she took advantage of his position to hop onto his back and clamber up and onto his shoulder. I'll admit to a moment's worry about how he might react to that. I had no idea if Billy was a cat person or not. Some people weren't. Take me a few weeks ago. I'd have run if I'd seen one coming at me. But then my allergies had a lot to do with that.

I shouldn't have worried. Billy handled her like he handled most people in his life. He turned his head to look her in her little kitten eyes and smiled.

"What do you think so far, Princess?"

Destiny tilted her head at him for a minute, then glanced over the supplies and tools he had already laid out in preparation for his day's work. Finally, she turned back to him. And licked his nose.

I'd take that as a sign of approval. Billy seemed to too.

We didn't really feel comfortable interrupting Lily and Opal's conversation, so after Destiny did her business in the small flower garden, while I stood guard and cover of course, we made our way back up the stairs. This time she demanded to be carried. I guess gravity was more of a factor going up the stairs, even for cats.

It was still early, but going back to bed didn't seem like a good option at this point. By the time I dropped back off to sleep, it'd be time to get up for real, anyway. Might as well make the most of it.

My eyes were drawn to the mystery novel on the end table by the sofa, but apparently, Destiny had other ideas. She made her way over to my backpack and stood there looking at me.

"What? Is there something in there that you want?" Then I shook my head at her. "Whatever it is will have to wait just a bit. I need to get you all set up first." That didn't take all that long. I put litter in the box and the box in the corner of the bathroom, and a food and water dish filled and sitting in the corner of our little kitchenette out of the way. The whole thing took maybe five minutes.

She was still sitting by the pack, staring at me. My little Destiny was a very determined kitty about getting what she wanted.

"All right, fine." I walked over and unzipped the pack, then dumped all the insides out. Geesh. I should probably do this more often. There were all kinds of things inside that thing. Some I didn't even remember putting in there.

After throwing away the empty water bottles and food wrappers, I started sorting through the rest of the items. There was my taser which reminded me that I should probably check in with Boswell Bonds to see if he had any new bail jumpers for me to go after. I could use the distraction. Besides, I was getting pretty dang good at it.

I felt the hair at the back of my neck go up, and a glance over at Destiny showed her staring at me again. She didn't look happy. In fact, she shook her tiny little head at me.

"What?" I was starting to think I'd be saying that a lot from here on out.

She walked over to the taser and rested one delicate little paw on it, then turned back to me and shook her head again. I felt my brows draw together.

"You don't like the taser? Or you don't think I should be a bounty hunter?"

Most cats probably can't smile. At least I don't think they can. Destiny can and did. Then she took her little noggin and pushed the taser off to the side.

I reached over and picked it up. "You might not like it, but this little device has saved my bacon a few times. A girl needs a bit of protection in the world nowadays."

Huh. What do you know? Destiny was really good at Opal's signature look.

What the heck was I in for here? Suddenly having a kitten that was part Goddess didn't seem like such an awesome idea. I'd need to be on my guard twenty-four-seven around her.

Then I realized, or just maybe Destiny beamed the thought into my head, that the Goddess had always been watching.

"Yeah," I told Destiny just in case the thought had come from her. "But you weren't so very demanding before now."

That got another kitten smile and Destiny turned and snagged a single piece of paper from my pack and dragged it over to me. She looked from it to me. I may be dense sometimes, but when the Goddess gives me a message as clear as that one, I listen.

The paper was the copy I'd made the day before of all the suspects in Ralph's murder investigation. At least the ones that Mabel and I had been able to come up with.

"Are you telling me that, out of everything I could be doing right now, you want me working on this?" I waved the paper at her. We would have to come up with some kind of system for communicating. The Goddess had more than hinted that we could go mind to mind if I allowed it, but I just wasn't sure I was quite ready for that yet.

I wanted to hold on to my sanity for a bit longer.

"How about this? When I ask you a yes or no question, you meow if the answer is yes and wag your tail if the answer is no. Would that work?"

Meow.

Okay, but I would need a little further clarification. That could totally have been a fluke, right?

"So, you want me to work on finding out who killed Ralph?"

Meow.

I thought for a minute, my eyes going over to the end table and my book. If this was just a fluke... well, it was worth testing out that possibility, anyway.

"How's about I take the morning off and just read and sip coffee?"

That didn't amuse her. Destiny's tail didn't just give a single wag, it began moving furiously. Obviously, the Goddess was used to getting her way.

I took a deep breath and stood and walked over to the sofa.

And yes, the paper was still in my hand. I could take a hint.

* * *

By the time my phone rang at a quarter till noon, I'd managed to get a pretty solid feeling for the Ralph situation. Of course, I'd had that feeling before I'd even started. Ralph Morgan was a scumbag of the first order. He'd deserved everything he got and probably a lot sooner than he'd gotten it. I couldn't feel one bit sorry for him. If that made me a bad person, so be it.

The only ones I felt sorry for were the ones he left behind and the mess they had to clean up because of him. Too bad whoever had killed the jerk hadn't taken the body and buried it in a deep hole far, far away.

But no. They had to leave the thing in plain sight for Mabel to find. Maybe the killer wasn't such a good guy after all. Not that I really thought that the killer was a good guy. Good guys don't kill other people. Even if I had come close to doing that myself before.

Really, really close.

I answered the phone, already knowing who it was. The Andy Griffith whistling tune gave Opie away every time.

"Hey, Opie, what's up?"

"You know, now that we're boyfriend and girlfriend, it might be nice if you started calling me by my actual name. That's Trevor, in case you've forgotten."

I thought about it. Didn't sound right, but I could give it a try. "Hey, Trevor, what's up?" Man, that sounded weird even to my ears.

"Thanks for trying, anyway. I was calling to see if you wanted to join me for lunch. There's a new chicken place opening up across from Boswell Bonds. I thought we could try it out."

Sounded good to me. "You buying?"

He chuckled. "Would I be asking if I wasn't?"

Fair enough.

"Then sure, I could eat some chicken." I felt a paw on my arm and looked down to see two little kitty eyes staring at me. "Just remind me to save a little to bring home for my cat."

"Leftovers? When has that ever happened between the two of us?"

He had a point. "Okay, then remind me to order another piece before we leave. I have a feeling things could go pretty badly here if I come home without some."

Meow.

There, see, I knew it.

"Not a problem. I'll even pay for Destiny's meal too. Just put in a good word for me with her, okay?"

"Deal."

I was getting ready to say goodbye, but then he spoke again. "Oh, and Amie?"

"Yeah, Op—Trevor?" This would take a major effort on my part.

"Would it be too much to ask you to ride your bike to meet me?" His voice sounded hopeful.

Again, he had a point. He was on a roll today.

"Sure. It'll take me longer though, so if you get there first, go ahead and just order me whatever you're going to have."

"Will do." And he was gone. Men were so abrupt when ending phone calls.

I'd still be saying good-bye right about now.

I shoved the paper back into my backpack, along with a few other necessities of life, but when I reached for my taser, it was gone. I looked all around the bag on the floor where I'd left it and in the bag itself. No taser.

Then I looked back at Destiny. She seemed very satisfied with herself.

The Goddess might not like the taser, but right now in my life, I felt it was a necessity to have on me at all times. If I got totally ticked off at a person, I'd have an alternative to use rather than having to rely on my magic. With the threat of the council looming over my head, using my magic in public simply wasn't such a good idea. A little spell from me could end up being ten times what I'd intended for it to be. That kind of thing draws attention.

Destiny gave an audible sigh. Yes, that's possible, because she just did it. Then she hopped down from the sofa and disappeared beneath it. Seconds later the barrel of the taser peeked out from under it.

I reached down and grabbed it and shoved it into my bag.

"Thank you," I said. There may have been a touch of sarcasm in my voice when I said it. I guess I should have been grateful that Destiny had decided to go along with my way of thinking.

Thinking.

I was halfway down the outside stairs when it finally hit me. I hadn't said a word about the taser, the magic, the council, none of it. I'd only thought it.

My cat could read my mind.

Goddess, but I was in so much trouble.

Chapter 12

T he brisk bicycle ride helped clear my mind from my newest startling revelation. So the Goddess could read my mind. Since when had that ever not been the case? She could read all of our minds and knew every little thing about us too. Even our most deep dark secrets were subject to the Goddess' gaze.

In reality, nothing had changed. It would still take a lot of getting used to, mind you. It's one thing to know that the Goddess is watching your every move, and a totally other thing to have a piece of her right there judging your every move and hiding your taser.

This would take a much bigger period of adjustment than I had planned on.

I pulled up outside the new chicken place and gazed for a minute up at the sign over the door. Clucky's Palace. Really? They couldn't come up with a better name than that?

It kind of made me wonder why Opie had wanted to meet here. Hopefully, their ability with food was a little better than their creative ability with name-giving. Then I saw the sign in the window.

Opening day special: Lunch Buffet half price. $3.99 today only.

Ah, that explained it. I hoped they kept the buffet well stocked. Opie and I could do some major damage to it pretty quickly.

Even with the special and prime location, the place wasn't nearly as busy as I would have thought it would be. Opie was there already and had snagged us a table fairly close to the buffet line. One of the best seats in the house, really. Close enough that it would only take a few steps to be able to refill our plates, but far enough away that we weren't constantly being interrupted by other diners doing the same thing.

I stopped by the table and dropped off my pack. Opie already had two plates piled high with food in front of him. I'd have to catch up.

"I've already paid for both of us, so go ahead and grab a plate."

The heck with that. I'd grab two. It might have been the lesser crowd, but there was more than enough food to fill two plates. I'd go back later for a dessert plate. The food looked good too. I loaded down with grilled chicken strips, mashed potatoes, steamed asparagus, and a roll that was almost the size of my head.

It smelled good too.

Opie got a full hour for lunch, and it was a good thing. Conversation lagged during the first half-hour as we were far too busy shoving food into our faces to talk. This place would definitely be one of our regular haunts. If they survived, of course. A lot of new restaurants didn't. Then again, it was going into the summer tourist season, so they might do okay after all.

When our bellies finally allowed us to slow down, Opie looked over at me. I noticed he was kind of blushing. It was enough to tell me that this wasn't just a normal lunch date. He had something on his mind.

"Spill it."

He took a deep breath. "I had a kind of weird dream last night." His blush deepened. "It kind of involved you."

I grinned at him. We hadn't taken our relationship to the stage that would create blushing yet. Maybe this was a good sign that we'd be getting there soon. I was more than ready. It was only the thought of my uncontrolled magic that had been holding us back this long. Well, holding Opie back, anyway.

"Not that kind of dream," he said.

Well, dang. "Then what kind of dream was it?"

Another deep breath. "I'm really not sure. This incredibly beautiful lady came to sit on the side of my bed, and we had a long chat. She told me that I needed to get you back into Karate. You know, like we used to do back when we were teenagers."

Yeah, there for a while we'd really been into it. Even did a few low-key cage fights. Don't judge. They were mostly for fun.

Mostly. When the fun part stopped, so did we. It just wasn't worth it.

That didn't mean we weren't any good at it. We were. Both of us. But when you're good, everyone wants to fight you to make a name for themselves. That's the part we could do without.

"You still got your belt?" We'd made it all the way to brown belt before ending our lessons. We probably could have gotten our black belts if we'd really wanted them. To use, though, it wasn't about the belts. Never had been.

"Yup. Do you? And more importantly, do you still have your outfit?"

That made me think. "I don't think so, honestly. It's been a while, and I've changed out my entire wardrobe too many times for it still to be there."

"I'll buy you a new one… and pay for our lessons too. The lady was pretty insistent. She said you needed the discipline right now."

I couldn't meet his eyes. I was thinking I knew exactly who this dream lady was.

"Did this lady happen to have long golden hair that fell in waves like liquid sunshine? And was she perhaps wearing a long flowing gown that looked like wedding night lingerie? Did she smell like the most expensive women's perfume ever?"

When I finally raised my eyes, I found him staring at me in horror.

"How the hell did you know all that?" Then he glanced around and lowered his voice. "Can you gals enter our dreams now?"

I laughed. "Oh, no, nothing like that. It's just that I had a visit from the same lady a day or so ago. Actually, she isn't a lady at all. She's a Goddess. The Goddess, actually."

He swallowed and continued his staring. His mouth opened a couple of times, but nothing came out.

I knew how he felt. She kind of did that to me at first too. Before she became an annoying little kitty presence in my life.

"So, when do we start? Have you decided what dojo to join?" I hoped that by getting back to the subject at hand, he would recoup faster.

It didn't work.

"The Goddess?" His voice squeaked a bit. "Please tell me you're kidding me."

He should know I wasn't. Otherwise, how the heck would I have hit the nail on the head with my description of her?

"Unfortunately, no kidding involved." I blew out a breath

and pushed what little food remained on my plate around for a few seconds. "She seems to be taking a huge interest in my life right now. I think she has big plans for me."

He lowered his voice even farther. By now, he was almost whispering. "What makes you think that?"

Um, she kind of told me so herself? A part of her was currently inhabiting my new familiar? I really didn't think he'd be able to process either of those things right now, even if they were both true.

I shrugged. "Well for one, she visited my boyfriend in his sleep." Then I giggled as I thought about it. "Please tell me you were wearing pajamas."

His color flared even more than it had before. That kind of answered that. I bet he'd be wearing them from here out, though.

"So, the town's dojo or are we going out of town for this?"

It had been worth a shot, even if it didn't work. The man could face down the criminal element on a daily basis to keep the town safe, but the simple thought of a Goddess seeing him naked had him totally derailed. That's my guy in a nutshell.

I switched tactics. Reaching around to my backpack, I drew out the list of suspects and my very meager order of suspiciousness. Marco Ramirez was at the top of the list. If that didn't get Opie's attention, I didn't know what would.

Yes, I'd given the list, minus my notes and numbering, to the sheriff already, but they hadn't known I'd kept a copy for myself. I was betting that would be enough to get Opie on a more solid footing.

I was right.

His eyes went from wide to narrow. "Why do you have a copy of that?"

"Because Mabel and Tommy are my friends, that's why."

Opie shook his head. "Let us handle this one, okay? I don't want you getting hurt."

For that, he just got the look. He had to know that just because he was a sheriff's deputy, that didn't mean I was okay with him getting hurt either. The buckshot he took from helping my family out still weighed heavily on my mind. He'd only just recovered enough to be put back on active duty. Personally, I'd felt a lot better about things when he'd been chained to that desk. Even if he did hate it.

"You know we do this for a living, right? We've gotten pretty good at it too."

I knew all that. His dad hadn't been the sheriff for the past decade just because of his handsome face and muscular body. Although, I'm sure that didn't hurt with the female voters in town. He was good at his job. And the town had never been safer.

"And you do know that once I get my license, I'll be doing this for a living too, right?"

He made a face. "Yeah, it's not like I will forget that little fact anytime soon. I'm kind of hoping you give up on that before then."

Like that would happen.

I snatched the paper back out of his hands. "I'm pretty good at this, too, you know." Especially with my family to back me up. But I didn't have to put that into words. He knew the power that backed me. He knew the power in me too. A little too well, actually.

Shoving the paper back into the pack, I tried for nonchalant. "Of course, if you guys already have a break in the case..."

He blew out a breath. "You know we don't." He paused for a

minute when the waitress came by to refill our drinks. Once she walked away, he looked me in the eyes. "Look, it sounds like this G—woman—was right. I think you need to brush up on your fighting skills. I remember you used to be pretty good. Have you kept up with any of it?"

"Without you knowing it? I don't think so. You pretty much know everything about me, you know. No secrets here." Not anymore, anyway.

He popped the last bit of roll left on his plate into his mouth. "I did, you know. Keep up with it, I mean. Did you know that?"

I stared at him. "Well, duh, you had to, right? Don't you like have to go to the gym for your job?"

Leaning back in his chair, he grinned at me. "You doing anything tomorrow night?"

"Nothing planned at the moment. You want me to pencil you in?"

"Make it in ink. This is an event that can't easily be rescheduled."

Something was up. He was looking altogether too proud of himself for my liking.

"Sure. Count me in."

"Good. I'll pick you up when I get off work." He started to stand, his lunch hour almost over. "Oh, and wear something you can move easily in."

Then he gave me one of his lopsided smiles and walked out. I watched him all the way to the door.

You probably would have watched him too. My man has a mighty fine backside view.

Chapter 13

What with the news of the Goddess invading my fellow's dreams and all, I totally spaced out on the whole getting an extra piece of chicken thing. Of course, now that I really thought about it, smuggling a piece of chicken out of the restaurant and then leaving it in the hot basket of my bike probably wouldn't have been the smartest thing to do.

And I had things to do while I was in town. People to visit. Starting with Marco Ramirez, Ralph's business partner. Or should I say partner in crime?

The two of them had gone in together and purchased an old ranch house a mile or so outside of town, in the other direction from the farmhouse, thank goodness. Zoning restrictions weren't as hard to bypass when you weren't directly in city limits.

Now the poor house was what they called a Cigar Club. The gist of the whole operation was that it was a place for men to go and enjoy the finer things in life. Oh, they did that all right, if rumor had it right.

According to the town's scuttlebutt system, there were two rooms in the back dedicated to clandestine meetings with women. Some of whom were paid for their time, if you get my drift. And the building's basement was said to house an illegal gaming den and off-track betting establishment.

So, all in the same place, a man could enjoy a fine cigar, play a hand of five-card draw, and have some fun with a hooker. The finer things in life indeed. Of course, the only part of that the two men had advertised was the cigar part. The rest they relied on word of mouth to get around.

From the number of cars in the house's yard, I'd say business was booming.

I wove my bike through the parked cars and up to the porch. Leaning it against the side of the wooden porch railing, I paused to look around. And to listen.

With most country houses, you could hear what was going on inside for the most part if you got close enough and tried to. I was plenty close, and trying, but I couldn't hear a dadgum thing. Part of the renovations the men had done to the house must have included a ton of insulation and maybe even a bit of soundproofing. Can't say I blame them on that. Not if all that really was going on inside.

Once at the door, I hesitated. I mean, do you just walk in, or do you knock? Businesses that ran out of houses always confused me on the entry protocol. Finally, I just reached down and turned the knob. If they didn't want people coming in, they would lock it, right?

The door opened into a large open space filled with couches. A few men were indeed camped out on the couches smoking smelly cigars. If they weren't paid to do that for cover, then I bet their wives appreciated them having a place other than home to stink up like that. I never got the whole cigar thing. But then, I'd never tried one, either. Maybe the smoke tasted better than it smelled? In my opinion, it would have to. Or else these men were totally nuts.

I searched out the place and finally located Marco getting a beer from one of the massive refrigerators in the kitchen area. He almost dropped the can when he saw me standing there. Good thing he hadn't had time to open it yet.

"Hey, Marco," I said, trying out a smile. I'd been working on my acting skills. I think I was improving.

He glanced over at the men on the couches, but they hadn't even seemed to notice me yet.

Striding over to me, he took my elbow and marched me right back out the door.

"Hey!"

"Don't have a cow, but if you're here to talk about what I think you're here to talk about, it's better to have that talk outside."

By this time, we were both standing on the porch and the door was firmly closed behind us.

"What if I was just here wanting to play a hand of cards?"

He just looked at me. "Try again. Unless you're here to smoke a cigar—which I'd be happy to sell you—then you've come to the wrong place. We ain't that kind of joint." His expression told me differently, but I wasn't here to argue with him. Not about that, anyway.

"Okay, so let's have that little talk then. Did you kill Ralph?"

Sue me, but I believe in being direct. What good did dancing around the issue do when we both knew why I was there?

Marco laughed. "Me? Kill Ralph? No way. Not until I got the money back from him that he stole from the business."

I gave a pointed look at the door behind him. "Cigar Clubs do that well, do they?"

"They can. If you know how to run them right. I do."

94

"How much do you think Ralph took?"

He glanced over to make sure the door was still firmly shut. It was. The soundproofing must work both ways. Even still, he lowered his voice.

"Around fifteen grand, which has really put me in a bind." Marco leaned in closer than I was comfortable with. "I think he was about to do a runner on his wife and needed the money to get away. I'd say she might not have been too happy about that if'n she'd found out about it. And he was killed right behind where she worked, wasn't he?"

I wasn't even going to respond to his implication. "Wouldn't that mean he was going to do a runner on you too? I'd say you wouldn't have been too happy about that, either. Especially with that much money missing."

"You got that right. And if Ralph was alive today, I'd throttle him within an inch of his life with my own bare hands, but as it stands, I won't be getting that opportunity." He paused. "But you gotta admit, his wife had motive. That money he took is somewhere. And if she finds it, well, she's the widow, right? No way will I ever see it again. She's the one you need to be looking at. Not me. Then, too, there's the whole insurance thing to think about."

"Insurance? You mean like life insurance?"

He shook his head. "No, but he may have had some of that too. Even more reason to look at Mabel, if you ask me. She's gonna come out smelling like a rose."

Marco hadn't really answered my question. "So what insurance are you talking about?"

"Business buy out insurance. Or they call it something like that. My missus insisted that me and Ralph did the business end of things right. We took out a policy so that if one of us died the insurance company would come up with half the business' worth so the one left could buy out the family's share."

I thought about that for a minute. "So, you get to collect half of what the business is worth?" The house alone would be a substantial chunk of change. I was starting to see a motive here.

"You ain't listening to me. The money goes to Mabel Morgan. It's all in the insurance contract."

That took a little more thinking on my part. "Okay," I said slowly, getting my thoughts around it. "But that means that now you own this place all by yourself, doesn't it? No more partner to have to share the profits with?"

He swallowed. "True, but it will take me a good while to make up that money Ralph took. It's not like I'm suddenly gushing with money cause he's dead. And I'll have to hire someone to help with the... operations too. That'll take money." Marco shook his head. "I still think the best bet is the wife on the whole murder part of things."

Then he winked at me. "Or maybe the little Trixie he was gonna leave her for. Can you think of any reason a woman would want a man like Ralph besides money? Maybe he gave that money to her, and she killed him so she wouldn't have to deal with him."

"You wouldn't happen to know who that was, would you?"

His lips thinned out. He knew all right, but he wasn't going to tell me.

"We're done here." And he turned around and went back inside. This time, I heard the lock click into place.

Fine by me. I had other places to be, anyway.

* * *

The way home took me right back through town. As I started past the library, I decided to stop by and see how Mabel was holding up. All of this had to be killing her. Plus, to be honest, I wanted to make sure that Tommy Hill wasn't hanging around. I knew he wanted to be there for her through this, but being seen together just wasn't the smartest of ideas.

At least I'd been worried about that for nothing. Mabel was alone at the front desk, and other than a couple of people reading in the big easy chairs, the place seemed empty.

"If you're looking for Clarence, he isn't here," Mabel whispered. "This is the day he takes the book van over to Shady Meadows Retirement Home. He won't be back until after we close."

"You okay here by yourself?"

She nodded. "It's better, actually. No one asking me questions about... everything, you know? I mean, the patrons want to, I can tell, but so far, they haven't. I appreciate that."

Yeah, Wind's Crossing might be small, but we had a lot of good folks. Most of the ones that frequented the library were the good ones.

Her words made me feel a bit guilty though. After all, I was there to do just that. Ask her questions.

She must have known that because she gave me a sad smile. "It's okay. Really. I can't ask you to help me with all this and then not tell you anything you might need to know."

"Thanks." I looked over my shoulder to make sure the readers were still in their chairs. "I just came from Marco. Do you have any idea where the money Ralph took might be?"

She shook her head. "Truthfully, I wish I did. Ralph didn't leave me in the best of spots financially speaking. The man had a gambling problem and being around it day after day...."

She sucked in a breath and looked at me.

"It's okay. I kind of figured the rumors going around town were true. It isn't news to me."

Mabel nodded. "I think everyone in town knows what really goes on there, but so far the sheriff hasn't made a move on them. Probably choosing his battles."

"But the insurance money will help you, won't it?"

She laughed, but there wasn't a bit of humor in it. "We barely had enough life insurance to cover his burial. There won't be enough left to catch up even the house payment." Her eyes grew watery. "I'm going to lose the house, Amie. There's just no way I can keep that from happening now. It's awful of me, but at first, I thought maybe Ralph had taken that money for us. To catch up on things. That didn't happen. I never saw a penny of it."

Marco might not have been so far off after all. It sounded like Ralph was gathering up resources to do a runner. And it didn't sound like Mabel was part of his plan.

"I wasn't talking about life insurance, though. I was talking about the business buy out policy the men had taken out."

Mabel tilted her head at me. "The what?"

I told her about the policy that Marco had informed me about. Her reaction surprised me.

She started laughing. And crying. Mabel leaned hard on the counter in front of her with her face in her hands. When she could finally catch her breath, she looked up at me. "Oh, Amie. You don't know how much that will help! I thought... I thought I was worse than bankrupt. To think that I can keep the house... maybe even pay it all off?" She sank onto the office chair behind the desk, shaking her head. "I just can't believe it. My prayers have been answered."

If she was acting, she was much better at it than I was.

She hadn't known about the policy, and she hadn't been part of the theft from the business either. My heart felt a lot lighter. I didn't like having suspicions about my friends.

But there was one more thing I had to ask her.

"Do you have any idea at all who Ralph's... lady friend was?"

"That's a nice way to put it, but no. I don't know who she was." She hesitated. "I'm pretty sure it was one of the two girls working the back rooms at the club, though. Ralph talked about them, but he would never give me their names."

There wasn't anything else I could think of to ask, so I left. Mabel was even smiling as she waved goodbye from the library's door. At least I'd taken one worry off of her.

Now to find out who really killed Ralph and why.

But first, I had a Goddess cat to feed.

And no chicken.

Chapter 14

No chicken meant a stop by the market before going home. I hadn't been prepared at all when Lily had dropped off Destiny.

As I wandered through the pet food aisle at the store, I came across some tiny cans of cat food that had cute little pictures of cats eating out of fancy dishes. Shoot, Fancy was even part of the name. How could I go wrong with that? Plus, as expensive as they were, they had to be good, right?

I loaded up a dozen cans into my cart and checked out. Full of the knowledge that I had done right by my cat. Goddess piece or no, she was a cat first after all.

The ride home was a little hotter and stickier than I liked. Having a car for those precious few weeks had really spoiled me. Now, I had a car but didn't want to ride in it because I'd reek for hours afterward. I had to figure something out there. And fast. Summer was coming early this year for sure.

As I put my bike in the little lean-to under the stairs, I heard someone talking in the backyard. The odd thing was that it was a single voice, not two or three.

Curious, I walked to the corner of the house and peeked around. It astonished me at how the gazebo was already taking shape. It had only been a few hours. How on earth had he gotten so much done in so little time?

Then I noticed the lump on his shoulder. A cute little furry calico lump.

Had I left a window open? Not latched the door? I couldn't believe that Ruby or Opal had just let her out to wander. I mean, there really were hawks and other kitten eaters out here. It wasn't safe for a kitten.

Of course, a kitten sitting on the shoulder of a muscular handyman should be okay. But that wasn't my point at all.

Taking a deep breath, I walked over to them. When you dread a confrontation with your familiar, it's a bad sign, by the way.

"Hey, Billy. How long have you had an assistant? I could have sworn I left her inside when I left."

He grinned over at me. "Don't know how she got out, but she did." He reached up to touch Destiny's nose. "Kind of glad she did, actually. I was going to go about this all the wrong way."

Shaking his head, he motioned to the rapidly growing wooden structure. "I've never been this productive in my life." Then he blushed and looked over at me. "Don't suppose you'd want to give her away or anything? I could sure use her."

"Sorry, Billy. She's kind of special to me." Then I thought. There was a third kitten that hadn't found a home yet. At least I didn't think it had. I'd have to make a call. "She might have a sister that still needs a home, though. Would you be able to keep a cat at your house?"

He nodded. "Mom always said I could have a pet if I wanted one." He smiled over at Destiny. "It took this little gal to convince me I did." He rubbed noses with the kitten. "Where you been all my life, gorgeous?"

I swear the kitten fluffed up for him. It would appear that the infatuation went both ways. I could have trouble on my hands.

Not that I was jealous or anything.

Well, maybe I was. Just a little.

Billy ducked his head and bent to pick up a piece of wood. "So, have you seen Mabel lately? I was wondering how she was doing in all this. I went by her place last night to check on her, but she wasn't home. I'm kinda worried about her."

"Mabel's fine, Billy. Or she will be. She's staying with me for a few days."

"Is she really okay?"

I thought for a minute. I'm pretty known for telling people like it is, and I really didn't see any reason not to do that now. "She will be, Billy. It's just that Ralph's death left her in a pretty tight spot with money and debt and everything. I just found out that she had been afraid she might lose her home. It's put a lot of stress on her. That, coupled with the murder... well, she's having a rough time right now."

He looked crestfallen. "You mean that Ralph's death might have hurt her even worse than he did?"

"Financially, maybe. But then again, she wouldn't have been in that tight of a spot if Ralph had been a decent guy who believed in taking care of his family." Billy still looked worried. "And we just found out that the cigar club had a type of business insurance. We are hoping it's enough to pay off her house so she won't have to worry about it anymore."

A shadow of doubt passed his eyes and then was gone. "I guess as long as it all works out in the end, that's okay. Right?"

He really seemed to need confirmation from me.

"I'd say so, Billy. She's just going to have a rough time for a little while. Probably until they find whoever killed Ralph. It isn't easy being under suspicion of your husband's murder on top of everything else."

Billy's mouth popped open. "No one could think she done it! Not Mabel."

I shrugged. "Sometimes nice people do bad things, Billy. It happens. Not this time, but it does happen."

He thought for a minute and nodded. "Thank you, Ms. Amie. I got some thinking to do now." He reached up and lifted Destiny from his shoulder. After giving her a final nose rub, he handed her to me. "I think she might be hungry. You'd better feed her."

"Meow."

I was starting to miss having Arc as my familiar. He hadn't been nearly so needy.

I had a bad feeling Destiny was trouble with a capital T.

Destiny, of course, demanded to be carried up the stairs. With the bag from the market, it wasn't the easiest thing to do. I'm a hold the handrail kind of gal. Finally, she gave another of her sighs and climbed up on my shoulder. Maybe my cat had a part of a parrot too. But it made the stairs easier.

Once inside our personal little space, the first thing I did was check around for a place where she could have gotten out. The door had been shut and locked, and all my windows were down and latched.

I found myself staring at the little self-satisfied and smug-looking kitten. "I don't suppose you'd be willing to tell me how you got out?"

Her tail started wagging. Well, no had been the answer I'd been expecting.

"Fine. But just be careful, okay? There really are dangerous things out there. I'm not just making it up."

She just sat there looking at me. For some reason, I felt like I needed more than that. "Promise?"

There was a brief moment of silence as she obviously thought about it. "Meow."

I just hoped a kitten took a promise as seriously as a witch did.

I put the few things I'd bought away but kept out a can of the fancy cat food. I'd even gotten a cute little fancy glass dish for presentation. Feeling pleased with myself, I popped the top of the can and dumped the food into the bowl. Then I set it down beside her and waited.

Nothing.

Well, not exactly nothing. She looked at it and then looked at me. If looks could talk, this one would be saying 'oh, heck no'.

"You realize that you're a cat, right?"

Her chin lifted and her little eyes narrowed at me. I swallowed. There was a lot of Goddess in that look.

"I-I'm just saying that you are currently in cat form, or whatever this is, and that a cat's form would require the proper nutrients for a… well, a cat, right?"

The stare continued.

I took a deep breath. "You aren't going to eat that, are you?"

The tail swished, and she turned her back to me. I couldn't get a much clearer answer than that. I switched tactics. What choice did I have?

"Look, I don't have much time before I have to go down for Opal's daily lesson, and I can't just ditch that to run into town and get you more people-type food. So, you will have to settle for something I have in the fridge or cupboard. Deal?"

She looked at me over her shoulder. This time I waited her out. Her move.

Finally, she stood and walked over to the fridge. I took the hint.

"I should warn you, I run a very lean kitchen. There isn't going to be much to choose from."

With that warning, I opened the door and started listing off the ingredients inside. "There's a few slices of bacon I could nuke for you, a couple of eggs that I'm pretty sure are still good, and a little shredded cheese leftover from taco night. That's it. Those are your choices." I paused. "When Arc was a cat, I'm pretty sure he went with bacon and a side of cheese. Would that work for now?"

"Meow."

Good. I'd hate to starve my poor little Goddess-ridden kitty cat. I talked as the microwave worked its magic. "Are you staying up here or coming with me down to Opal's for the lesson?"

She just looked at me. I waited. It was a legitimate question. Then I realized that while it was a legitimate question, it wasn't one that could be answered yes or no.

"Do you want to go with me?"

"Meow."

This would take so much getting used to.

Chapter 15

I totally blame Destiny for us being late.

After she ate, she needed to use the litter box. My gentle encouragement to hurry the heck up wasn't taken well. I would have left without her, but I feared the repercussions from such a heinous act.

As it was, it was three minutes past three when we reached the bottom of the stairs. Opal was standing in her doorway with one eyebrow raised. Then she looked down at Destiny and raised the other one.

"You do know it isn't necessary to bring your familiar with you, don't you?"

I shrugged. "Since I haven't had her up to now, yeah, I kind of figured it wasn't necessary." Then I pointed down to the furry little creature. "Try telling her that, though."

Was that a smile? If so, she hid it quickly.

"So, what's on the docket for today's lesson?"

She opened her mouth to answer but before she got it out, we heard a car coming down the driveway. At speed.

I followed Opal out onto the porch and was a bit shocked, not to mention worried, when I recognized the vehicle as Patricia Bluespring's car. Other than my aunt Opal, council members scared the heck out of me.

Okay, scratch that. All council members scared the heck out of me. But at least I knew Opal was on my side.

When she climbed out and then reached back in to bring out a small cat carrier, a little of my tension eased off. Maybe this wasn't about the Light Witch thing after all.

In fact, Patricia seemed quite distressed. She nodded at Opal and then turned to me.

"I'd appreciate having a little chat with you if you could spare the time."

Yup, her voice definitely held a great deal of tension. She looked like she was about to drop the carrier, get back in her car, and drive away. I was starting to think I had a handle on the why of her visit.

I looked over at Opal. "Would you mind if we started the spell lesson a bit later?"

She gave a grunt. "Already late as it is." But she had to have noticed Patricia's discomfort too. "Why don't you come inside, and I'll get us some drinks."

"Do you have anything with alcohol? Vodka sounds really nice right about now."

Opal raised an eyebrow and nodded. "I think I can handle that."

Once Opal had gone in the front door, Patricia turned back to me, her eyes more than a bit wild. "Can we talk in front of Opal?" Her voice was barely a whisper. Not that it would matter. Opal had the ears of a... well, whatever animal could hear really, really well.

"This is about your new familiar, isn't it?"

Patricia swallowed. "Yeah, I'm thinking they aren't just ordinary cats."

She wasn't wrong.

"You could have something there." I thought for a minute. I didn't really feel right hiding the whole Goddess in my cat thing from my family. I figured the kitten would have to leave the bag sometime. Might as well be today. "With us living right here under the same roof, I don't think I should really hide it from her, do you?"

"You've got a point."

"A very good point," Opal said from behind me. "What the heck are the two of you going on about?" Then she looked at Patricia. "The vodka's in here by the way."

We went in and settled in Opal's sitting room. She had the front curtains drawn back, and the sun lit up the room with its bright rays. And heat. Opal must have seen my expression because she walked over and turned on her big floor fan.

"Better?"

I nodded. "Thanks." I chose a seat in the fan's breeze, and Opal poured out two glasses of Vodka. One for her and one for Patricia. She knew me well enough to know that wasn't my drink of choice. Especially not the straight stuff she kept on hand. I was more into fruity drinks. And soda. I loved my soda.

"So, did you come here to tell us that big secret of yours that the Goddess warned us about?"

I swear to the Goddess, if it had been anyone but Opal, I would have thumped them on the back of the head. This was so not about that.

Patricia almost strangled on the sip of vodka she'd just taken. "What... the Goddess... what?"

I wasn't all that sure which part of Opal's question Patricia was having the most trouble with. The secret part or the Goddess warning part. It would appear Patricia wasn't so sure either.

"This is about something totally different, Opal." I gave her a rather scaled-down version of the Ravenswind look. "This is about our new familiars. They're kind of special."

Opal locked gazes with me. "How special?"

"Very, I'd say. But it appears that Amie knows far more about than I do."

Well, yeah, the Goddess had told me.

"Can I ask why you're here, Patricia?" I asked. "What happened?"

She took a shaky breath and set her glass on the coffee table. "I found myself overly tired this afternoon for some strange reason, so I took a nap. And during that nap, I had a very vivid dream."

Opal groaned. "Oh, please, just let me take a wild stab at this. A breathtakingly beautiful blond woman wearing a long flowing see-through gown and smelling like heaven on earth?"

Patricia's eyes got even wilder. "How the… are you guys messing with dreams?"

That was the second time someone had accused me of that in the same day.

"No. But that's how Amie described the Goddess when she visited her in her meditation sanctuary. I kind of figured she'd be in the same guise when she visited you." Opal looked up toward the ceiling. "You know, after more than a couple of dedicated decades as your high priestess, it might be nice to get a visit every now and again from you myself. Now that I know you do that kind of thing."

"Meow." Both kittens went off in stereo. It was almost eerie. What the heck am I saying? It was eerie as heck.

All eyes went to them. Destiny walked over and very calmly

109

released the latch on her sister's kennel.

"How did…"

"Breathe, Patricia. Breathe," I said. "I think the kittens want to tell us something." I looked over to Opal. "And when either one of them talk, I think we would be smart to listen."

"They talk?" Opal's voice did something I'd never heard it do before. It squeaked.

"Well, talk might not be the best word. But I'd say we should do whatever it is they want us to."

Which appeared to be to follow them to the front door. Patricia bent down to scoop up her kitten and got a kitty smack for it.

"I don't want her to get away."

I looked down at Destiny. "She won't run away, will she?" A tail wave. "You're absolutely sure?"

"Meow."

I looked back up to the others and found them staring at me in horror. What could I say?

"You have Destiny's word that your kitten won't leave us." It sounded weird even to my ears, but that's the truth of it.

Patricia's mouth was moving but nothing was coming out. Opal was just staring at me. That hadn't changed. She was waiting.

"Why don't we follow them and see what they are up to? I have a feeling that would be much better than me trying to explain something I don't fully grasp myself."

I reached out and opened the door and the kittens shot out as if maybe we'd change our minds. For a second, I was worried that they had played me. But they stopped at the corner of the house, turning to us to make sure we were following them.

We did.

Billy was just packing up when we reached the rapidly growing meditation gazebo. He grinned when he saw the kittens running toward him.

"Hey there, Princess! You bring a buddy to see my work?" He scooped them both up and nuzzled them to his face. Both cats reciprocated. Big time.

"You done for the day, Billy?" Opal asked. "I think we might need the spot if you are."

"Yup, just getting ready to take everything out to the truck. I'll be back tomorrow first thing in the morning if that's okay with you." He hesitated. "How early do you ladies get up? Wouldn't want to wake you all with my hammering."

"Any time you get started will be fine with us, Billy."

He might not be able to tell it, but Opal's voice was strained to the breaking point. We helped him carry everything out and put it away in his truck just to speed things along.

Once we watched his truck disappear out onto the main road back into town, we returned to the gazebo. The structure was already framed and half the floor had been installed as well. Unfortunately, half wasn't enough room for three people to fit comfortably.

We'd have to improvise and sit on the ground. But Destiny and her sister weren't quite ready yet. Destiny made a beeline for the stairs and then looked back at me. Maybe I should invite her to share thoughts after all. It would make the whole communication thing a whole lot easier.

"You know, it might help if I knew your cat's name," I told Patricia. It might be a bit disrespectful to keep thinking of her as the other cat.

"Athena." Patricia was staring at the little white bundle of fur sitting patiently on the gazebo. "I'm beginning to think that was more than a fitting name for her."

"Oh, I'd say that is definitely the case."

"MEOW."

"Hold your horses, I'm coming." I turned to Opal. "Once I do whatever mission of urgency Destiny is sending me on, do you want me to grab pillows for us?"

She nodded. "That would be nice, dear." When I turned to walk away. She said, "But do please hurry, dear. If I'm guessing right about where this is going, I've waited a very long time for it already."

Then a few more minutes would not kill her. But, of course, I didn't say that. I just gave her a nod and ran over to Destiny who was sitting at the bottom of the stairs waiting for her ride.

When we got to the top and inside the tiny entrance hall, she turned her head pointedly toward Ruby's door. Uh-oh. Arc was still in there and things were awfully quiet. I really didn't want to have to interrupt them.

"Is this really necessary?"

"Meow."

So be it. I knocked. There were definite sounds coming from inside now, mostly just shuffling about. When Ruby opened the door, her hair didn't look quite as perfect as it normally did.

"What?" She put a lot of force behind that word.

"Your presence is being requested down in the new meditation garden. Ouch." The ouch was because Destiny caught me with a claw as she jumped from my arms. I watched her as she darted into the apartment between Ruby's feet. "I'm thinking maybe she wants Arc too."

A muffled meow came from inside. At least I was getting better at reading my cat's intentions.

"Who is requesting?" She didn't sound like she was so convinced it would be worth her while.

"Your mom for one, but I think she's actually on the lower end of the scale on this one."

Ruby's eyes widened. "Give us two minutes, and we'll be down."

The door closed, then re-opened a second later. She handed me Destiny, and the door closed again.

Now to hunt up some pillows that I didn't mind getting grass-stained.

Chapter 16

B
y the time I'd gathered the pillows, collected Arc and Ruby, and made it back to the garden, Opal and Patricia had already started without us. That may very well have been part of the Goddess' plan.

Oh, she probably did want Arc and Ruby in on this monumental meeting, but she probably also wanted a chance to have the older two witches alone for a few minutes. She accomplished both in one fell swoop.

I felt kind of bad that Mom would miss this. She deserved to be in on it too. But she was a fairly lengthy drive away. And like I said, they'd already started without us. No way would they have waited for Mom too.

It took a little while for me to get into my trance state. The others beat me, most likely by a matter of minutes or more. I really had to buckle down on my practicing.

I had thought I would be on the path to my sanctuary. That's where I normally end up. The trees looked familiar. Although they should, because I used the path up through our woods to the Gemstone Coven's meeting circle as a model. But when I came to the clearing, it wasn't my sanctuary before me.

Which I guess stood to reason as I was joining a meeting already in progress. You have to invite people into your sanctuary. It's part of why it's called a sanctuary. You were in control of everything that went on there.

Unless, of course, the Goddess decided to show up. She was the one being in all the universe that didn't require an invitation.

I had a strong feeling that this was her sanctuary. Or maybe, just her home. Whichever, it was incredibly breathtaking.

At the center of the back of the clearing was an enormous tree. Far bigger than any I had ever seen in real life. At least in my home state of Michigan.

But it wasn't your ordinary tree. Far from it.

The front half of the tree was open. Or maybe the sides of the trees curled around to the front just enough to make it appear open. And within that opening were dual staircases. One led to the right, and one to the left. Each led deeper, into the tree itself. It was incredibly hard to try to put into words, but the effect was nothing less than stunning.

A sanctuary fit for the Goddess.

The only problem was that I wasn't quite sure which stairway to take. The left or the right. Then I heard a definite meow coming from the left. That answered that.

As soon as I stepped onto the first step, time and space seemed to warp around me and suddenly I was sitting in the same room as the others. If you could call it a room. It was rather like sitting in a roofed forest surrounded by color and clear white light. If peace were a place, this would be it.

"Took you long enough."

I glanced over toward Opal's voice and was pleasantly surprised to see Mom sitting beside her. For some reason, that made my heart a lot lighter. I really hadn't been comfortable about excluding her from such a momentous occasion.

Opal and Mom were sitting on the Goddess' right and Arc and Ruby were on her left. Patricia and I were front and center before her. It kind of made me wonder why we were given the places of honor, but then our kittens came and crawled into our laps. Reason enough, I guess.

"I'm afraid this meeting can't last very long, but I wanted to gather you all together just this once to show you all that this is very real. There can be no doubts going forward. Are we clear on this?" The Goddess looked to each of us in turn. "Anyone in need of further proof that this is real? Or that I am the one you call upon?"

Silence ruled.

"Good, then we can get on with business. You should know that I don't have favorites among my followers. Not really. But with that being said, some of them are very special to me. I include all of you in that number. Some of you have unique talents that none other in our small circle possess. Others of you are compliments to those talents." She paused, letting that sink in. "That doesn't make any of you more important than any of the others. You are to be a team. My first team of Guardians."

"My Goddess?"

She turned to Opal, smiling. "Somehow, I knew you would be the first with questions, my priestess. What is it you wish to know?"

"What use can you possibly have of us? You are the Goddess. All is within your power. How could we be of help?"

The Goddess hesitated. "My power is legion, yes, but not without its limits. For instance, I cannot truly meddle in the affairs of mankind. Not on an individual basis. No matter how unfair I see things going—I'm not allowed to intervene. That is why I need you."

"But who is stopping you? From intervening, I mean?"

I was glad that Aunt Opal was taking the lead as our spokesperson. So far, she was doing a bang-up job of it as far as I was concerned.

"It's complicated, priestess. As my witches, you know that there are... other beings besides myself. Beings that do not have the best interests of man or mankind at heart as I do."

Opal nodded.

"The rules of the universe are somewhat keeping them at bay. For now. That would change if I began acting in ways I should not. If I became personally vested in the welfare of humans, that would open a door for them to do the same. Only welfare would not be their aim."

I swallowed. Okay, I definitely didn't want that. It kind of explained a lot of my questions growing up, actually.

"What do you need of us?" Mom asked softly. "I believe I speak for all us when I say you have only to ask."

The Goddess' smile graced us all. I could feel the warmth of it covering me like an electric blanket on the coldest of winter's nights. It felt like everything would be okay.

"There is no one thing. Merely to continue on as you are. Battling injustice as you find it and fighting for the good in people. There are people who need your help. Desperately." Her eyes found mine and held them. "Your current path is a good one. Study and learn. Your lessons will be needed. Magical and legal. There is corruption in my council."

I felt my breath quicken. Surely, she wasn't going to pit us against the council. Especially if she couldn't help us in the fight. We'd all be slaughtered. Except maybe me. I'd be the Energizer Bunny for them for the rest of my life.

"No. I am not asking you to take on the council. Not yet. I just needed you to know the reason I am turning to you rather than to them."

It all sounded good except that not yet part. That had me more than a little worried.

The Goddess tilted her head to the side. "Ah, I'm afraid you have company, my children. They will grow worried if you remain unresponsive. Amie, before Patricia leaves your home, take her for a stroll around your house. She can be of help to you. Now, I'm afraid, our time is at an end."

"Wait," Patricia begged. "I have to know about Athena..." But she was talking only to us.

We were back in the garden. And we had company as the Goddess had warned.

Mabel stood to the side of the half-built gazebo, staring at us.

"Would someone mind telling me why your cats are glow-ing?"

"Holy Moly! You mean the spell worked? I didn't think it would." Arc didn't miss a beat. He glanced over at the kittens and then seemed to be disappointed. "Ah, but it's already fading, dang it. Not a very long-lasting spell then."

Mabel looked confused. "That was a spell? But why would you want your cats to glow?"

Gee, I wanted to know that too. Arc didn't disappoint.

"Well, me and Ruby are working up a magic act for the kids at the hospital. One that, you know, really involves magic. We thought it would be kind of cool to have our animal assistants glow." He shrugged. "Not much good, though, if it only lasts for a minute or two."

He was way too good at this. He had me believing him, and

I knew it was just a line he was feeding her. Still, the magic show sounded like fun. Maybe we should all do that for real.

Mabel didn't look all that convinced, though. But at least she didn't argue the point. "Okay, then," she said, that trace of doubt still in her voice. "Well, I'm going to go upstairs now and take a shower." She turned to me. "Is it all right if Tommy comes over again tonight? He offered to bring Chinese food if you say it's okay."

Oh sure, bribe me with food. When has that ever not worked? Not that I would have said no, anyway.

"That's fine, but we'll need to make sure he brings enough for four. Tonight's movie night for me and Opie. He'll be here around seven if Tommy wants to come around then too." And my turn to pick the movie too, so it should be a good one.

"Cool." She seemed relieved. Maybe me giving her and Tommy all that alone time last night hadn't really been what she wanted after all. Maybe she wanted other people around at first. I could understand that.

She left, and I turned to Patricia. "I'm not sure what you can help me with, but I'm ready for that walk around the house if you are."

Patricia picked up Athena and nodded. "I'm curious too."

"Hell, let's all go," Opal said. "I'm dying to know what that was all about."

It didn't take long to figure out.

As soon as we turned the corner, my car and all its smelly fragrance was right there in front of us.

"Why do you have my neighbor's car?"

Chapter 17

The rest of the evening passed better than I could ever have imagined. Most of that was because Patricia lifted the hex she'd placed on my cute little bug and now it was odor free. Come to find out, her neighbor had run over her familiar one night when coming home after a night of drinking and partying. That isn't something any witch would take lying down.

The hex had been a strong one with an ingrown element to compound with every effort spent to reverse its effects. As a multitude of people had tried to erase the scent, it had grown greatly in size and magnitude. A hex is a far worse thing than a simple karma spell. And, now that I knew the circumstances, this one had been well-founded.

Besides, all's well that ends well. I got a great car that I never would have been able to afford otherwise, and Patricia's neighbor hadn't gotten nearly the value in the trade in that he should have. It all rounded out.

Though she still teared up when she looked at the car. Memories die hard.

After that, Arc and Ruby ran into town for more Chinese as they had decided to join us for the movie. We moved everything downstairs to Mom's and had a great time with everyone getting to know each other a little better.

I was especially happy to see Opie and Arc semi-bonding. It would be good if the two of them could get over the whole first meeting when Opie had tackled him to the ground and tried to arrest him. Hopefully, we were past that now.

Just after ten, the guys all headed home. Well, at least two of them did. I was kind of glad when Ruby asked Arc to stay the night. I had promised to give him a ride home when he was ready, and I really didn't relish the thought of being out on a long round trip road trip this late at night. I didn't have all that much experience driving at night, and right now the deer were running rampant. The last thing in the world I wanted was to take a risk of crashing my now odor-free baby.

I had fun plans for her. Plans that didn't include reacting to the phone call I got the next morning.

When the sheriff's ringtone woke me up, I just knew it couldn't be good news. He never calls with good news. In fact, he hardly ever calls. Usually, he leaves it up to Opie to hand-deliver any messages from himself. Generally, messages like stay off the case or whatever.

"Hey, Sheriff Taylor, what's up?"

"You free for a couple of hours? We could use you and that fancy camera of yours."

That didn't sound good. I swung my feet off the bed and onto the floor, feeling around for my slippers. "Where do you need me?"

He gave me the address, but it didn't sound familiar. That, at least, was good from my point of view. It meant it wasn't one of my friends. After that my heart released its clutch a little. Might not be right of me to think that way, but the thought of having to take death shots of one of my friends didn't appeal to me in the slightest.

And I was sure it was a death. They had never asked me to photograph any other kind of crime. At least not yet.

"Oh, and just so you know, I went to bat for you with the town council. Starting today, if I call to ask for your services, you'll be paid for helping us out. Consider yourself a contract employee." He paused. "There's probably some kind of paperwork you'll need to sign too. I'll have to look into that."

He sounded distracted… and worried. That, in turn, worried me.

"Paid or not, I'll be there, sheriff. Give me fifteen minutes."

"Make it sooner if you can. We need to get a jump on this one. Fast."

And he was gone.

* * *

There was a very good reason that the address Sheriff Taylor had given me hadn't rung any bells. I'd never been to the Metal Mansions Mobile Home Park before.

It was back off the main road and obviously, I'd never had a reason to travel down the little gravel road leading into it. Good thing too. It was a depressing place. There were twelve homes in total and whoever named the place must have been high on crack or something. I'd seen mobile homes before. Some of them could come close to earning the title mansion.

Not these. Every last one of them was rundown to the point of being one tiny step away from condemnation. It hurt my heart to think that people actually lived in them.

That part was obvious though, from the throng of people milling around outside the yellow crime tape barrier. None of them seemed super upset, either. So, either the person who'd been killed wasn't a village favorite, or they were so used to seeing police presence here that it just didn't excite them anymore.

Either way, it was kind of sad.

Opie saw me and pointed over to where their police vehicles were parked. I pulled up behind the last in line and got out, picking up my camera from the passenger seat first.

Taking a few deep breaths, I tried to center myself before I reached Opie and his dad. This was never easy. Even if it wasn't my first time. I didn't think it would ever get easier, even after I'd done it a hundred and one times. Some things never do.

The look on both their faces told me this was something big and my heart lurched.

"Oh Goddess, please tell me this isn't a child." I'm not sure at all I could handle that.

Sheriff Taylor shook his head. "No, it's a man. Pretty much the same as Ralph Morgan, actually. Appears to be stabbing wounds in his chest and stomach. Ninety-nine percent sure that's what killed the man." He jerked his head toward the trailer within the tape's boundaries. "He's in there. His bedroom is the one to the right."

I nodded and looked over to Opie. After a quick glance to his dad, he led me in.

"So, what's the story?" I asked when we were a few feet away. "Who found him?"

Opie nodded over to a little girl, probably around ten or so, standing off to the side with a woman's arm around her shoulder. "His daughter. He'd been on another bender last night, and she'd been afraid to go home, so she stayed with a neighbor. She snuck in this morning to get changed for school."

"If she was trying to sneak in, why did she go into his bedroom?"

"She said something didn't feel right, and she thought maybe he was waiting for her. She wanted to make sure he was asleep and not ready to pounce on her." His voice was oddly monotone. "He wasn't known for being a good father."

I let that sink in as we climbed the short set of steps and crossed into the trailer itself. The inside was pretty much what I expected. One larger area served as both a living room and kitchen. There was a door to either side that I figured had to lead into the bedrooms. I turned to the right and entered the man's room.

As I started snapping pictures from as far away as I could, Opie filled me in a little more.

"The girl's teacher called us yesterday, and we had a talk with Mr. Jefferson here. Not that it did much good. I guess after we left, he hit the bottle twice as hard. Lucky for little Nancy, the neighbor was on the lookout for her and snagged her before she made it home. Who knows what the man would have done to her. Maybe killed her this time."

I swallowed. "Why did the teacher call you?"

"Nancy showed up for school limping. A visit to the school nurse was pretty damning to Jefferson. The girl's body is mostly covered in bruises. Places you can't see, of course, with all her clothes on. Typical for an abuser."

He was still talking in that monotone. It wasn't like him at all. He was feeling this one hard. And it wasn't the man lying dead in his bed that he was feeling for.

I stopped snapping and looked over at him. "You okay?"

Opie nodded, then lowered his voice to barely a whisper. "I

will be. Thing is, I'm beginning to think this killer is doing us all a favor. And feeling like that has me scared. A cop can't go around thinking a double murderer is a good guy."

I pushed the lump out of my throat, but it took a couple of tries. It didn't go easy. Call me slow, but I hadn't put the pieces together that far yet. "The same killer? Wind's Crossing has a serial killer?"

"Worse than that," Sheriff Taylor said, stepping into the room behind Opie. "It looks like we have a vigilante killer."

"How is that worse?"

The sheriff looked at me with grim eyes. "Because sometimes towns have been known to rally behind the vigilante. Sometimes one or two will even try to get into the game in the name of taking back the town from the bad guys. It's not a pretty picture."

Taking back the town. I'd heard that phrase just recently. Actually, I heard that phrase most times I went to the library. Crazy Al.

Opie poked me. "Get back to snapping. The coroner will want in here soon. Not that I think his job is crucial in this case."

"Oh, it's crucial all right." The sheriff said. The monotone thing was catching on. "He'll be able to tell us if it's one killer or two." He rubbed a hand down his face. "Right now, truthfully, I don't know which news would be worse."

I finished up in the bedroom, getting shots of every angle that I could think of. When I was done, I went into the living room and started in there. The window in the bedroom hadn't been large enough for a man to climb through. A child maybe, but even that was doubtful. It was more likely the killer had entered by the front door.

Opie followed me, watching me in silence. When I'd managed to get the whole area covered, I glanced at the door into the other bedroom. The one closed door in the whole place.

"Do you want pictures of her room?"

He hesitated, then nodded. "Yeah, better to be safe than sorry."

I opened the door, and I think a little bit of my heart broke. If I hadn't been standing right in the threshold between rooms, I would never have believed this room could be in the same trailer. It was a far cry from the rest of it.

It was clean and tidy. The furnishings were modest, but the girl had gotten hold of some dowel rods and an old sheet or two and had fashioned a canopy for her tiny twin bed. Pictures of castles, dragons, and royal princes and princesses abounded. A lot of them were hand-drawn and colored. It was a room of innocence.

A room of a girl who wanted desperately to be in a land far, far away.

Chapter 18

When I'd gotten done at the trailer park, I'd headed straight back home. Running upstairs, I grabbed my fuzzy, furry bean bag chair and dragged it out onto the balcony.

Billy was already hard at work below on the gazebo, and I didn't want to interrupt his work. But I needed the fresh breeze on my face. I needed all the comfort the Goddess' world could give me right now because I couldn't get that little girl's room out of my mind.

Nancy Jefferson had a hard life ahead of her, but just maybe it would be a better one now. No foster home could be worse than the one she'd been raised in. Could it?

I pushed the thought from my mind and settled into the chair, closing my eyes.

Mom had suggested before that I set up a trigger sequence to get myself ready faster for the trance state. I didn't have time for that now, but it was something I acknowledged that I desperately needed. I wanted to be in my sanctuary sooner rather than later.

Unfortunately, the events of the morning were fighting hard against my mind finding the peace it needed. Then I felt a soft warm lump jump into my lap, and I was there.

The tension and heartbreak fell off me in waves as I walked the short path to my little piece of heaven. By the time I reached it, I felt whole again. I was half expecting the Goddess to be waiting for me.

She wasn't. Then her words from the day before came back to me. I couldn't ask her directly about this case, or any other. She wouldn't be allowed to answer. If she started giving us privileged information about the bad guys, or possibly over-zealous good guy in this case, then the bad entities out there could start giving our secrets away to the really bad guys.

That way lay madness. No, I was on my own.

But that didn't mean I was out of options. This was my sanctuary after all. I could invite anyone I wanted in. Past, present, dead, or alive. All were fair game here. Of course, it wouldn't actually be them appearing, but my sub-conscious brain wouldn't know that.

It was better than nothing. I thought about it. Who could help me best in this situation?

Then a stray thought hit me. I wondered if the invitation would work for a fictional character. One who had never drawn breath in the real world.

It was worth a shot, right? That opened up all kinds of possibilities, but the one my brain zeroed in on was none other than the greatest detective of all time. Sherlock Holmes.

I was kind of surprised when it actually worked. There, before me was a tall and slender man wearing a trench coat with wings of a sort and his signature hat. He even had a pipe.

The man glanced down at his outfit and laughed. "You honestly believe this is the way I dress?" He waved his hand and now he was dressed in jeans and a leather bomber jacket, then seconds later the jacket disappeared to be replaced with a simple pullover turtle-neck sweater.

"Ah yes, that's so much better." He glanced at me. "You don't know how very annoying it is to be immortalized in an outdated outfit that in reality no man ever would have been caught dead in."

I grinned at him. "Tell that to all the guys who dress up like you at costume parties. They love it."

"Yes, well, just wait until the fashion police catch up to them. Times do change, as I'm sure you are aware."

He looked around pointedly, then back at me. "There doesn't appear to be anywhere for me to sit. Am I to stand during the interview?"

Crapsnackles. I really wasn't very good at this. I concentrated and a plain brown leather wing-backed chair popped into existence across from me. I waved to it, feeling very accomplished. I was getting the hang of this, by golly.

He nodded, then took a seat. Only then did his eyes rest on my chair of choice. His laughter was immediate and long. Very long. Long to the point of becoming very annoying long.

"Excuse me, but in case you are wondering, I like this chair and I really don't care what you think of it."

It was a struggle, but he managed to contain himself finally. "Agreed." The laughter was still in his voice, but I could handle that better than the other.

"So, if I may ask, why do I suddenly find myself in such a... unique... place?"

"I need help. There have been two murders in my little town, and I just needed someone to talk it out with."

"Ah, so the game is afoot." Then he paused, frowning. "Did I ever really say that? It doesn't sound like me at all."

"I'll have to re-read the stories to be sure, but yeah, I think you did. Quite a lot to be honest. It's a catchphrase now that people just connect with you."

"A pity that. I shall have to choose my words more carefully from here out, I suppose." Then he leaned forward slightly, his eyes widening slightly. "So, tell me the details."

A part of me knew that I was just taking myself back through both deaths in my own mind for my own purposes, but I did just what he asked. I started from the beginning of getting the call from Mabel and brought him all the way up until now. It took a while because I didn't want to leave anything out. I felt that was important. Who knew what astounding clue I may have missed that he would now jump on to solve the case with a nice and tidy little red bow.

When I stopped, he leaned back in his chair, reached into his pocket and drew out a match to light up his pipe. A split second before touching the flame to the bowl, he looked to me. "Do you mind?"

I shook my head. "Go for it." I might not like cigar smoke in the slightest, but I always thought pipe tobacco was kind of sexy. Not that I found Sherlock sexy. Although… no, I had to drag my thoughts back onto target. No rabbit hole traveling today. I was on a mission.

"Well," he said finally, after a quick puff on his pipe. "I'm guessing that the police are already questioning this Crazy Al you spoke of? Of course, he would be the prime suspect after his abundant sermonizing on taking back the town."

Yeah, well, tell me something I didn't know. That's what you're here for. But I didn't say that. It wasn't nice to be rude to guests you had invited into your sanctuary. Even if they were nothing more than figments of your imagination.

I waited.

"Unfortunately, in my experience, the perpetrator of the crime is rarely the first suspected of it." Another fragrant puff. I'd have to see if it listed anywhere in the stories what type of tobacco Sherlock used. It was rather intoxicating. In a good way. Could be useful in spell work. Or simply as a kind of odd potpourri.

"So where should I start?"

He raised an eyebrow at me. "Well, a good detective—or even someone such as yourself with time on their hands—might begin by going back to that list of suspects you spoke of. Perhaps someone on that list has a connection to both men?"

I felt my mouth drop open. Now this was more like it. Not that I appreciated his words about my lack of ability as a detective, mind you. I forced myself to let that slight pass.

"Do you have any particular suggestion as to where to start? Does any of them seem to stick out to you as more suspicious than the rest?"

Now the other eyebrow rose. "I would hardly be a good judge of that, as I know none of the people on that list. One would need to do a little investigative work to ascertain any possible connection."

He had a point.

Then he stood, brushing down the front of his pants to dislodge any wrinkles that sitting may have caused. Yeah, like he was used to wearing jeans.

"So, was there something else you required of me?"

"Not that I can think of at the moment." I paused. "Would you be willing to come again if and when I need you?"

That got a brilliant smile. "Oh yes, I quite look forward to it."

I guess I expected him to simply disappear, kind of like his sudden popping into existence, rather in reverse, but he didn't.

Instead, he walked out the front threshold of my sanctuary and down the tree-lined path.

For just a second, I wondered if I had just set a slightly modernized version of Sherlock Holmes loose into the world at large. Then I realized that we were still firmly encamped in my mind.

And having the greatest detective of all time camped out in there couldn't be a bad thing.

Could it?

* * *

I did a little legwork and found my first connection pretty quickly. Which could actually turn out to be connections, as in plural, since the main binding factor appeared to be the cigar club.

As it turned out, it wasn't the wealthy and well to do men folk in town that frequented the club. It was more the scummy underbelly of men—well, you get my meaning. The club was a place for men to spend money they couldn't afford to spend in the hopes of striking it rich on a great hand of poker. Like that would happen.

But it didn't stop them from trying. Apparently, the basement card den also made a small killing on serving alcohol. No liquor license, either, so I was rather hoping a police raid would shut the place down sooner rather than later. Get these men back home to their families where they belonged.

Then I thought about Jefferson and his daughter. Maybe spending time there rather than home wasn't such a bad thing after all. It might give the family a much-needed break. But the alcohol supply still needed to be stopped. That didn't help things one bit. But shutting down their little illegal bar wasn't my main mission today.

Today, I was staking out the place to try to find out who the women were that worked there.

I'd already made Marco's acquaintance, and while I could believe he would kill Ralph in the heat of the moment over the missing money, I was having a hard time putting him in the role of murderer for Jefferson. If the man owed money to the club, I could understand breaking a kneecap or something, Godfather style, but dead men didn't make good on their losing bets.

But the women? They were a different story. People might think a woman wouldn't choose to kill a man by stabbing him. I wasn't all too sure about that. Especially if the man had no reason to fear her. Maybe because he knew her in every sense of the word?

Neither of the men had exactly been lightweights, but then both had been found in comprised situations by the killer. At least that appeared to be the case.

Ralph had been taken down to the ground by Mabel and Tommy, and Jefferson had likely been killed in his sleep. Another reason to suspect a woman killer, in my opinion. Most of us women knew the stack was dealt against us, strength-wise. It made sense to wait for a better opportunity.

I pulled a bottle of water from my pack and took a sip only to spray water everywhere when a hand touched my shoulder.

"What are you doing here?" Opie asked, kneeling beside me in the grass. And here I'd thought I had chosen my hiding spot well. Bushes covered me from just about every angle.

"Besides having a heart attack and watering the bushes, you mean?"

He gave that lopsided smile. "Yeah, besides that."

I jerked my head at the club. "What do you think I'm doing?"

"I think you're treading on an official police investigation involving not one but two murders." His hand ruffled through his hair. "You need to go home, Amie. Let us handle this one. Please?"

I thought about it, then remembered the Goddess' words. We were her army now. No, that wasn't right. We were her guardians. As such, it was as much up to me as it was to the police. Not that the police would understand our jurisdiction.

"I'm sorry, Opie... I mean, Trevor. I don't think I can." I patted my pack. "But I've got my taser, and I'm ready for just about anything."

He just looked at me.

"Okay, so you scared me. Bully for you." I paused. "How did you know I was here?"

"Your car is pulled off down the road. Where else would you be this far out from town?"

Reminder to self. Next time make a bit more effort to hide my vehicle.

"You know I could take you in for obstructing the police, right?"

"Huh, really? Me just sitting here in the bushes minding my own business is keeping you from doing your job? In what way?"

He blew out an exasperated breath and gave up, finally settling in beside me on the grass. "Well, for one, you took my spot."

Oh.

"Sorry about that. But I'm more than willing to share." I scooted over closer to the bushes on the right to give him more room. "I kind of figured you and your dad would be focused on Crazy Al right about now."

"Dad is taking care of that angle of things. But I don't think it's him. Might be someone that takes his words to heart a little too much though. That's what Dad is trying to find out. Who Al's biggest admirers were."

"And you ended up here." What do you know? Me and Sherlock had been right, coming to the same obvious conclusion that the law enforcement had. Kind of made me feel a bit of pride. I could so rock this investigation thing.

"Yeah, well, don't get all full of yourself because you beat me here. We have other things we're looking into too."

"Like what?" I was going for a friendly conversational question, but he wasn't biting. Instead, he laughed.

"Sorry, kiddo, you'll have to get there on your own." Then he sobered. "But I really do wish you'd sit this one out, Amie. If Dad is right, and we're talking about a vigilante, it could get pretty ugly pretty fast. I'd rather you weren't at the heart of it when that happened."

I thought about it for a minute. "But if it is a guy or girl just trying to clean up the town, wouldn't that mean I was actually safer? They wouldn't hurt someone that wasn't on their list, would they?"

He shook his head. "Don't count on that. For one, they might start thinking about the old saying that you have to break a few eggs to make an omelet." He leaned forward and kissed the top of my head. "I don't want my little egg to be broken."

Ah. He almost had me. Almost. But I didn't want my big egg broken either.

"And what's for two?"

He took a deep breath. "I'm not so sure that Dad is right. I'm thinking we might just be talking a run of the mill serial killer."

"Any connections you found between the two victims besides the club?"

"Nice try, but I didn't answer the other variation of that question, and I'm not going to answer that one either."

I shrugged. Me and Sherlock would find them if there were any. Just give us time.

A car pulled in and parked in the building's somewhat busy yard and a woman got out. A woman showing a whole lot of skin. I pulled out my binoculars and focused in on her.

Jean Pratchett.

"Where did you get those?"

I handed them to him. I'd seen what I needed to. For now, anyway.

"That's Jean, isn't it?"

"Yup. Must have decided to make the most of her kids being in school and her husband being at work."

I shivered. I would never have thought her capable of selling herself like this. You really didn't know what people could do, did you?

"Not someone I expected to see here," he said, starting to hand me back my binoculars, then pausing. "Mind if I keep these for a bit?"

The thought crossed my mind to rub in the fact that I had them and he didn't, but for just this once I let it go. "Sure. But if another woman shows up, you have to tell me who they are and how long they stay, okay?"

He considered that and then nodded. When I started to stand into a stooped-over position, he looked confused. "You mean you're actually going to do what I asked and go home?"

"As it happens, yes. Opal's expecting me. But I'm holding

you to your word about telling me if another woman shows up. You agreed."

"That was before I knew you were leaving."

Like that mattered.

"I don't suppose you have another bottle of water and maybe a granola bar or something in that pack of yours?"

I dug out a small heap of comfort food and a bottle of liquid refreshment, then kissed his cheek and started to leave. Then I remembered that we had a date for that night.

"Are we still on for tonight?"

He grinned up at me. "Oh yeah. And remember the comfortable clothes. Yoga pants and a T-shirt would work great."

"Where are we going, the gym?"

His grin got bigger, but he zipped his lips and threw away the key.

Yeah, real adult.

But then so was sticking out your tongue at someone.

Chapter 19

I got home with ten minutes to spare. That was early, dang it.

Far too early to find my aunt Opal outside on the porch with her purse resting beside her in the swing. It took that sight to make me realize that her car wasn't parked out front where it should have been.

"What's up, Opal?"

She looked at me with troubled eyes. "No lesson today, Amie. And I have a favor to ask you. I loaned my car to Ruby and Arc, and now I need to go into town. Could you please give me a lift?"

That stopped me in my tracks. Aunt Opal rarely asked for favors. Especially from me. I must really be improving for this to happen.

"Sure thing." Then I glanced at the house. I'd drank a lot of water in my short time on the stakeout. "Could I take a minute to use the restroom first?"

She nodded, and I ran. I was back, and we were headed down the drive in less than three minutes. That's when it hit me that I had no idea where we were actually going. Opal must have realized that too.

"If you could take me to the sheriff's office, please, and wait outside for me a bit, I'd greatly appreciate it."

I stole a glance at her. "Not a problem. Can I ask why, or is this a secret meeting?"

"No secret. The sheriff told me you helped out with the pictures at the trailer park this morning, so you know what happened there."

"I do."

She looked out the side window, not meeting my eyes. That had me worried. Please, Goddess, don't let Opal have done another karma spell. Or worse, two.

"The foster parents they use for temporary housing for children are at their capacity. There isn't any place to send poor Nancy. Sheriff Taylor reached out to me, and I agreed to take her in."

The car swerved as I jerked my head toward her then back to the road. "How do you think the town will feel about a family of witches taking in a poor, innocent little girl? Won't they think we'll corrupt her with our evil ways?"

Opal grunted. "The townsfolk that think like that can go get themselves stuffed. The girl needs help right now, and there isn't anybody else stepping up to the plate to give it." She hesitated. "Probably just as well too. Nancy has shown traces of real talent. I've been watching her for a while now."

Then why was I just now hearing it?

"Does she have ancestral power?" Most true witches, the ones with real magic, came from a long line of witches. Generation upon generation of them. Like us.

"Not that I'm aware of, no. But not every birth is written in the books. Especially when it comes to the fathers involved. A few sneak in that we don't find out about until later. The earlier we get to them the better."

I thought of what the girl had been through, and it was enough to create more than a little of worry. "You know she's likely to be pretty messed up." I paused. "If you've been watching her, then you know her father was abusive, right?"

She continued staring out the window. For a long moment, I thought she wasn't going to answer me.

"I knew. But the sheriff said there wasn't anything we could do. The child protective services got involved at one point, but she fell through the cracks. Not nearly enough manpower to help all the children who need it. Something needs to be done about that."

I swallowed, not without difficulty. "You didn't, did you?"

Finally, she looked over at me. "Didn't what?"

"Do something about it. In Nancy's case in particular."

"No, Goddess help me, I didn't. But I'm not saying that thought didn't cross my mind. I know that murder is an awful thing, but I can't help but think that the world is a better place without those two men in it. Now, maybe, Nancy has a real chance at life. At least, if I have anything to say about it."

Two very different thoughts hit my brain at the same time, causing me no little distress. The first was that the sheriff just might be right about the town rallying behind the vigilante killer. If that was the case. I would even admit to feeling a bit the same way myself. Right or wrong didn't really come into it. The men simply deserved to die. Which kind of left me in a moral quandary. Maybe the rest of the town as well. At least I wasn't quite ready to light my pitchfork on fire and join in. Hopefully, none of the other people in town would reach that point either.

The other thought was a more personal one. That one won out in the end.

"So, bringing Nancy home isn't a temporary thing?"

Opal was back staring out the window. "Only time will tell on that one. But I will say that I'm open to that."

Good to know.

* * *

Normally, going into the Sheriff's Station didn't bother me much. Maybe because I have friends who work there.

Today was different.

I couldn't stop thinking how very scary this place had to be to a girl that hadn't even hit her teen years yet. Not to mention the fact that she'd already been put through the wringer today. I couldn't imagine what she must have felt when she found her father. Sadness with a touch of relief? At least she wouldn't have to worry about coming home to a beating for no other reason than her worthless father had lost another hand at the cigar club.

That didn't change the fact that she was now an orphan. Opal had told me before we got here that Nancy's mom had died at childbirth. Yet another reason for Jefferson to treat the girl like dirt instead of a person, I guess. As far as I could remember, I don't think I'd ever met the man in life. I was kind of glad of that now.

Opal had said I didn't have to go in with her, but I did anyway. Nancy had been through enough, and I know how intimidating my aunt can be even at the best of times. I was hoping me being there would help put the girl at ease a little.

Imagine my surprise when the girl ran into Opal's arms and the hug was immediately returned. I think maybe Opal had downplayed just how much she'd been 'watching' the girl.

"Thank you for agreeing to do this, Opal." Sheriff Taylor stood from behind his desk and walked over to us. Then he looked at me. "I had a female deputy go over to their trailer and start packing up Nancy's things. If you could swing by there and grab them on your way home, I'd appreciate it."

The girl shivered in Opal's arms.

"Maybe I should go after I drop her and Opal off at the farmhouse," I said, watching the girl shake.

"Even better." He reached out to touch Opal's shoulder. "I put in a rush on the paperwork to get you registered as a foster parent, but it will take time. You ready for that?"

She nodded. "Will there be a problem with me keeping her at the farmhouse until the forms get pushed through?"

He rubbed his chin. "I shouldn't think so. If there is, I'll do everything in my power to make it go faster. I can't really promise you more than that."

"I understand." Opal pushed the little girl back just enough so that she could look into her eyes. "Are you ready to come to the farmhouse, Nancy?"

The girl nodded, then looked over to me as if asking if that were okay by me. I smiled at her.

"I think you'll like it there, Nancy. And I have a funny feeling my new kitten is going to really take a shine to you." I wasn't lying. There was something about the newly orphaned that brought out the Goddess in all of us. Destiny would probably not let the girl out of her sight for a few days.

But that reminded me. "What about school?"

The sheriff smoothed down his mustache in a scratching type motion. "I've talked to her teacher, and I don't think that will be a problem. There is only a week left of school before summer break, and Nancy here is quite the smart little girl.

Missing one week won't hurt her."

"Can I get the stuff out of my locker?" The girl's voice was soft and very hesitant. Like she was jinxing something by even asking.

"I'll make sure of it," the sheriff said.

I noticed the girl's shoulders relaxed a little after that. Then I realized that her school locker was probably the safest place the girl had to keep things important to her. The things there probably meant much more to her than the few items I'd seen in her room.

And when you think about how tiny those lockers are, that was an incredibly sad thought.

We all piled in my tiny bug. Opal surprised me yet again by squeezing herself into the back seat with Nancy. I was seeing a whole new side of my aunt lately. It looked like maybe I'd been wrong about the kind of unbending person I'd always thought her to be. But then, I was growing by leaps and bounds lately too. That could well be part of it.

Maybe I was just seeing her out of wiser eyes.

When I pulled up at the farmhouse, Opal turned to me. "Why don't you show Nancy around—give her the grand tour, so to speak, while I fix things up inside a bit?"

Nancy didn't look so sure about leaving Opal's side, but whatever Opal had planned, there was a reason for it. When I saw Lily's van pull into the drive with both her and Mom in the front seat, I kind of guessed what was up.

"Maybe you two could start by exploring the backyard and the upstairs, and then join us downstairs in oh, say… an hour?"

Nancy took a deep breath and nodded, but her head was down. I could tell she really didn't want to be with strangers right now. I didn't blame her. The world of strangers is a very scary place when you didn't have a family that had your back.

I put my hand gently on her shoulder. "Let's start with our new meditation garden. Billy Myers is building a gorgeous gazebo for us."

She jerked her head to look up at me. "Billy's here?"

A few seconds of listening confirmed that. "Sure sounds like it. I take it you know him?"

Nancy gave me a timid smile. "He's nice to me. Sometimes Dad forgot to put money on my lunch card, and I guess someone told Billy about it. After that, every morning when I went to school there was a brown paper bag on my desk with a note from him." The color rose in her cheeks. "The food was nice, but the notes are what really helped."

Ah. Unless I was mistaken, there was a little bit of schoolgirl crush going on. That was fine, but I'd need to have a talk with Billy about it. He'd have to know not to encourage her.

When we rounded the corner, and he came into view, she called out to him. When he turned, his eyes lit up when he saw my companion.

"Nancy! I've been so worried about you." He jogged over to us and gathered her up into a big bear hug, actually picking her up off the ground. "When I heard what happened, I tried to find you, but no one would tell me where you were." He put her down and knelt down in front of her. "I'm so sorry you're the one what found him." He started to say more but stopped himself before the words came out.

Her eyes were welling up with unshed tears so I changed the subject back to something a lot nicer. There would be plenty of time for tears later. Probably for a long time too. But right now, the girl just needed a little breathing room from her grief and pain.

"How's the gazebo coming, Billy? I wanted to show it to Nancy."

He looked up at me, startled, like he'd forgotten I was even there. He recovered quickly though, and stood, holding out one hand to Nancy. "It's almost done. Come see."

I let the two of them lead, following close behind. When we got to the structure, which was indeed practically finished, Destiny was waiting on the step up to the shelter.

From where I was, I couldn't really see the girl's expression, but I heard her quick intake of breath. "Is that your kitten? She's beautiful! I've never seen one with so many colors before!"

Nancy ran up to her and Destiny did her part by meeting her halfway. By the time my much slower pace caught up to them, Destiny was cuddled in Nancy's arms. The girl seemed much more relaxed now. Holding a small little furry piece of the Goddess could definitely do that to a person. Relax them right down to a puddle on the ground, if they weren't careful.

"Her name is Destiny." I hesitated, then figured it was okay to go on. I was quite sure that Nancy knew we were witches. And I was positive Billy did. "She's my new familiar, and she's very special."

The girl nodded. "I can tell." Then she grew a little sadder. "I've never been allowed to have a pet. Would it be okay if, while I'm here, I pretended she was mine?"

"Meow."

For once that wasn't Destiny talking. I glanced behind us and saw a very familiar tiny black shape strolling over to us. The third kitten sister. The one the Goddess had other plans for. Seemed more than fitting to me. Especially if Opal was right and Nancy truly was a witch with power.

145

And one thing I knew from a lifetime of past experiences was that Opal was very rarely wrong.

Chapter 20

The little black kitten was a huge success. The instant Nancy's eyes fell on her, she handed me Destiny and scooped her up instead. Instant and total love quickly followed.

I really hoped that if we weren't allowed to make a more permanent home for Nancy here, that her next home would be open to having a tiny kitten come along with the deal. But then, with the Goddess involved, that was pretty much a surety.

With our kittens safely held to our chests, we finished our short tour of the backyard, and then I took them all upstairs to my apartment. Her eyes were growing bigger with every passing minute.

"How many people live here?"

"Right at this moment, we're back to four." I counted them off on my fingers. "Me, my cousin Ruby, Aunt Opal, and you."

She looked up at me. "Me?"

I smiled at her. "Right at this moment, yes." I hesitated to tell her that Opal was trying to make that a bit more permanent. I didn't want to get her hopes up. "And even if that changes, you'll be welcome here anytime at all."

"Really?"

I nodded and crossed my heart. She might not know it, but I

don't take that lightly.

She seemed to like my apartment, and she really loved my furry chair. I'd have to see if Ruby could get another one. We were still a long way from an hour-long tour, so I popped in some microwave popcorn and we sat to watch a short television comedy.

Although, truthfully, I think we watched the two kitten sisters playing more than we watched the television.

I was getting more than a little curious about exactly what was happening below us, so when I heard the van leaving and Opal called up the stairs for us to come on down, we were more than ready.

Nancy hesitated. "Is it okay if I take the kitten?"

"I kind of think that was the plan all along. Just for the record, she's as new here as you are." I thought about it. "Actually, you beat her here even."

"She came with the people in the van, didn't she?" Nancy was hanging back. At first, I didn't understand her reluctance to go downstairs, but her words kind of cleared that up for me.

"Yes. Lily was watching her for us. But unless I'm sadly mistaken... no, I will let them be the ones to tell you." I smiled down at her. "Come on. Let's go see what the old ones have been up to."

When we stepped into Opal's sitting room, I could barely recognize it. They had transformed it into a much nicer version of the girl's bedroom at the trailer. To include one of the twin-sized four-poster canopy beds from Mom's new home back in Oak Hill.

One entire side of the room was made up into her bedroom. Bed, small bookcase, portable wardrobe, and a rainbow-colored version of my fuzzy bean bag chair all laid out and ready for her.

"So, what do you think?" Opal asked. "Did we do okay?"

Nancy seemed speechless for a few seconds. "All this is for me?"

"Absolutely. And yours to keep, too. We'll go shopping for some books for your bookcase one day this week. And maybe for a few more clothes to fill that wardrobe out with too."

Now the tears did come. In earnest.

The girl ran over to Opal and buried her head in Opal's chest. Opal patted her head and made soothing sounds for a minute. Then she looked over at me.

"I know I've kind of usurped your whole day, but would you mind going to the… going to pick up Nancy's things? I'll take her to the school tomorrow to collect her locker stuff. But she will need some of her things tonight."

I nodded, dashing the moisture out of my own eyes. "I'll make it quick."

And I did too. I was back with my mission accomplished in under an hour. Good thing too. I only had a few short minutes to change and get ready for whatever the heck Opie had planned for the evening.

Keeping that mysterious thought at the forefront of my mind was the only thing stopping the tears from flowing.

I really hoped we got to keep her.

* * *

I was listening hard for the sound of Opie's muscle car. When I heard the sounds of tires on gravel, I ran down to meet him. I'd taken his suggestion and was dressed in simple stretchy black yoga pants and a black T-shirt. The perfect outfit if I decided to revisit the cigar club after our little get together. I still had one woman's name to uncover. I was kind of thinking maybe Jean took care of the day shift and the other woman had the nights.

Both women were still in my sights. I hadn't given up on them yet. Although, after getting to know Nancy a little better, I was starting to totally understand the whole vigilante thing. The bad thing was, I think I was kind of on his (or her) side of things. And I didn't think that was such a good thing.

It couldn't be good when one started rooting for a double murderer, now could it?

Opie grinned at me as I slid into his passenger seat. "You ready for tonight?"

"Bring it on. As long as you keep my mind occupied, I'm up for just about anything."

That sobered him. I should have kept my big flap shut. He glanced at the house.

"How's Nancy doing?"

I took a deep breath before I answered. More to center myself than anything. "As well as can be expected, I think. Opal pulled out all the stops to try to make her feel welcome. And she has a kitten now, too." That last bit would probably be the girl's saving grace. Not that Opal wasn't doing everything she could too.

"Good. Then let's go have a little fun." He reached into the backseat and handed me a blindfold. "Put this on."

I looked at it and then at him. "Tell me you're kidding."

The grin was back. "Nope. I want this to be a total surprise." He paused. "Besides, the location is kind of secret. The people we're going to meet kind of insisted on this. So... put it on, already."

There were other people involved? My curiosity spiked off the charts. But I put the dang thing on then turned in his general direction. "Are we good now?"

"Yup."

I could feel the car moving and hear the gravel, and I tried to keep track of which way he turned and the distance between turns. There was more than one way to figure out where we'd gone than just seeing it. Unfortunately, he must have figured out what I was doing. After all, we watch pretty much the same movies. He knows all my tricks.

The radio came on and music filled the car. That pretty much took care of me hearing anything important. Then he started talking. "Oh, and by the way, the other woman that works there didn't show up while I was watching. But I swear half the men from town go to that place. Marco must be making a killing."

"You know they serve alcohol without a license, right?" I hated not being able to see him. Was he shocked or did he already know that?

"We've heard rumors, yes. Unfortunately, no one has made a formal complaint and we really don't have enough evidence to initiate a raid warrant."

Too bad. Personally, I'd love to see Marco and his business taken down. They were a blight on the whole town as far as I was concerned.

"Any word on the vigilante angle of things? I know you all have talked to Crazy Al by now. Learn anything juicy?"

Silence. I started reaching for the blindfold, but his hand grabbed my arm.

"Look, Dad has me on a pretty tight leash on this one. I've been told to really limit what I tell you, okay? Give me a minute to work things out where I can tell you without, you know, telling you, all right?"

I could handle that. It took more than a minute though for him to work it out.

"Did you know that the night Ralph was killed there was a big shindig just outside of town? A band of hard rockers set up a camp type music festival a few miles out. Seems that old Al found out about it. Instead of informing us, as he should have, he decided to try to make some converts." A slight pause. I could totally imagine him shaking his head and running a hand through his hair. But then he did those things on a regular basis. "It didn't go all that well for old Al. He ended up in the hospital over at Oak Hill. A concussion from hitting his head after being pushed off his milk crate and a couple of broken ribs. They ended up keeping him overnight."

In other words, Crazy Al had a rock-solid alibi for Ralph Morgan's murder.

"You guys really think the killer is the same one or is there a possibility Al really has gathered a small army to do his work for him?"

A groan. "You aren't making this easy on me, Amie. Give me another minute."

The minute stretched into two, maybe even three. Not being able to see a clock, there was no way I could be certain.

"I got nothing. I can't think of a single way not to tell that the coroner thinks the same murder weapon is the same in both murders. So, you get nothing from me, understood?"

"Understood." So, Al wasn't our guy. That didn't mean it wasn't one of his converts though. Or that he didn't know exactly who it was. I was getting ready to head down that conversational path when I felt the car stop.

"We're here."

I felt his fingers slip under the blindfold and lift it. I blinked a few times to get used to being able to see again. Sight is a pretty powerful thing.

He leaned over and kissed me softly. "Whatever happens tonight, I want you to keep in mind that I love you. I'm doing this because I want you to be safe, okay?"

All right. Now my curiosity took a nosedive into worry. What the heck had he planned? An intervention of some kind? What the heck had I done to justify that?

Opie got out and came around to open my door for me. I spent the few seconds that took to look around. We were parked off a little access road—probably somewhere in the forestry that ended where Wind's Crossing began. But that forestry was huge. No way would I ever be able to pick this place out again. It was just trees and a small road. Those abounded here.

He took my hand and led me down a short walking path maybe a quarter of a mile into a clearing. What I saw there took my breath away.

My loving and caring boyfriend had brought me to a cage fight.

And I had a funny feeling I knew who the star attraction would be.

Me.

Chapter 21

"Please tell me you aren't expecting me to fight you in that cage."

I know the doctor had released him back to full duty, but I still wasn't sure he was ready for such strenuous activity. Cage fights weren't the kind that had a lot of rules. Or any rules for that matter. Of course, if I was his opponent that wouldn't be an issue. No way would I hurt him.

"Of course not."

I released the breath I'd been holding. Good. I'd read the situation wrong.

"You'll be fighting her." He pointed over to a woman who was standing with her back to us. When she heard his words, she turned to face us.

My heart skipped a beat. Missy Daniels. As far as I knew, and trust me I knew, Opie had only ever dated one girl in his entire life before me. Missy Daniels. Knowing now what I didn't know then, things made a little more sense. Like why I'd never much cared for the girl. From the feeling I was having at the sight of her, things hadn't changed on my end.

Then I realized she was wearing a brown deputy hat. What the hell?

She sauntered over to us. There was really no other way to

put the way she walked. She was definitely working the hip movement for the guys surrounding us. And there were a lot more guys than gals in that small clearing. About a six to one ratio from a quick headcount. Twelve men and just the two little old females.

"Hey, Amethyst, long time no see."

Not nearly long enough for me. I forced a smile.

"I thought you moved to the big city. Are you visiting friends?" Please, oh please, say yes.

She laughed and tipped her cap at me. That darn deputy cap. Opie and I would be having a long discussion about this later.

"Actually, I'm back for good. Been through the academy and now I'm working on Sheriff Taylor's team." She gave Opie a light punch on the arm. "Me and Opie will be teaming up for a week or so. He's going to show me the ropes."

A very long discussion.

"How nice." I was really testing out those acting skills that I didn't have. But I really don't think I was fooling anyone. A primal part of me wanted to take her down right then and there.

Then Opie's words came back to me. I guess that was the plan after all. And it would be sanctioned too. No one would think badly of me... as long as I could tamper down the instinct to pull her gorgeous red hair and not succumb to the urge to gouge her beautiful green eyes out.

Yes, she was a looker. That was more than a little part of the reason I really didn't like her. At all.

I turned to Opie who suddenly wasn't looking so sure of himself. As I said, I really didn't think I was fooling anyone. "So, you arranged all this, did you?"

He swallowed but nodded. "It's been a long time since we did anything like this, and I wanted the chance to see how much you retained from our dojo days."

I might have been happy about that, as it sounded like a reasonable plan to me, if only my chosen opponent wasn't my one and only arch enemy. Even if I was the only one of the two of us that knew that.

"You ready for this, Amethyst?" Missy asked, grinning. "I'd totally understand if you wanted a few days to prepare for it." She glanced around at the men still watching us from the sidelines. "Or maybe a year or two."

The smile I gave her now was real enough, even if it wasn't a very nice one. "Oh, I think I'm ready."

In fact, I'd never felt more ready for anything in my life.

Opie pulled me to one side, out of earshot.

"Can you do this without magic?"

Oh, now he worried about that? A little too late for that if you asked me.

"I've got better control now." I shrugged. "I'll do my best, but I really can't give you a solid guarantee you know."

"Maybe this wasn't such a great idea after all."

"You think?" Then I glanced back at Missy standing there flirting with the guys. They seemed more than happy with that. "Why didn't you tell me she was back?"

His eyes widened. "You mean you didn't know? She's been back for almost a month. I thought sure you'd heard the news by now."

"Let me guess. She came to town right after that thing with Opal, didn't she? What did she do, nurse you back to health? Is that what took you so long to get back to me?"

Opie took a step back. "Whoa. That isn't what happened at all, and you know it. I just needed time to process the whole magic thing. It's not like it was for all that long. Maybe what, a week total?"

The longest week of my life, but yeah, that sounded about right.

"So, you didn't spend any time with Missy during that week? Just hung around home thinking about my new powers?"

I could tell by his wild eyes and bouncing Adam's apple that wasn't the case. I turned back to the group behind us.

"Let's do this."

"Amie…"

But I kept walking. I was more than ready now.

* * *

I ducked into the cage opening and gave a little finger wave to Missy to signal that I was ready whenever she was.

The cage itself wasn't actually a cage as such. It was more a padded fencing that came in modules that could be put together on site easily. The fence came up to around my chest, but I'm on the short side. For a lot of the men milling around waiting for their turn in the cage, it would reach stomach level at best.

So, a motivated person could get out of the cage if they wanted to. It wasn't like you were actually locked in or anything. At least not by anything other than your pride and your opponent's aggression.

The real problem with these portable setups is the size. A regulation cage is much larger, giving the opponents room for footwork and the dance as they call it.

There wasn't any room for that in this one. Smaller cages meant hotter and faster fights. Right now, that was more than okay with me.

Missy stepped into the cage with a huge grin on her face. We'd see how long she got to keep it.

In hindsight, getting into that cage with a dozen or more witnesses and limited control of my new found magic probably wasn't the smartest thing I'd ever done. But as it turned out, I wasn't even tempted to use my power. My hurt, anger, and jealousy fueled my fight by more than enough.

When the referee gave the word, Missy came on in a rush with her hands and feet flying. I let her take me down three times. Sure, I'd wake up tomorrow with bruises galore, but it was worth it. A good fighter learns their opponent's strengths and weaknesses as quickly as they can. As I'd never before seen her fight, it took me a while to put it together.

The third time I bounced up from the mat, things changed. Big time. The gloating look on Missy's face didn't last long after that.

I couldn't afford her the same opportunity she'd given me to learn how I fight. I took her to the mat. Hard. She didn't bounce up as quickly as she should have, and it didn't take long to get her into a fierce hold.

There were three ways to win a cage fight. One was to knock the other opponent out. A clear win there. Another was if the opponents were more suitably matched and a knockout didn't happen in the allotted time frame. Then it was a matter for the referees to decide with the number of strikes and takedowns by each fighter. The third was something else altogether.

A tap out. An admission of defeat. In my experience, it was the loss that every cage fighter dreaded the most. That was the one I was going for here.

With her in an unbreakable and highly uncomfortable hold, she really had no choice in the matter. She could tap out and end this, or she could wait until the time ran out. Either way, under the circumstances, I'd be the clear winner.

Still, it took her a good three minutes of trying before making the tap. Another few seconds and a final small squeeze before I released her.

When she got up, the smile was gone. Her green eyes flashed for just a second as she glared at me. Where had I seen that before? That sudden animalistic flash. She didn't give me much time to place the other occurrence before it was gone.

Missy pushed by me without shaking my hand as custom usually dictates and made for her car. A low rumble started among the men. Hopefully, that meant they saw her for what she really was. A sore loser among other things.

I ducked out of the cage and stood outside. I wasn't happy to see that Opie had followed Missy to her car. Another point against him in my opinion. If I'd known where in the heck I was, I would have called for a ride home.

As it was, Opie was my only option.

That didn't mean I had to actually talk to him.

The ride home was a very silent one. After a minute of trying to explain, Opie finally gave up. He knew me as well as any other person on the face of the earth. When I was this mad, which didn't happen often, it was far better for the person who caused my anger to just shut the heck up.

I'd get over it. Eventually. Maybe. I was still really ticked that he had followed her to her car. Kind of a camel and straw kind of thing to me.

He barely stopped the car out in front of my house when I opened the door and popped out. He was ready for that. Maybe he wasn't as smart as I'd given him credit for, because he caught up to me before I made it to the outside stairs.

Grabbing my arm, he whirled me around to face him and his lips hit mine with a pent-up passion of years. It startled the hell out of me. Not what I was expecting at all.

But it did the trick. It broke my cycle of anger.

Within seconds, I was responding to him, pressing against him for more.

When we finally pulled apart, he smiled down at me. "I just couldn't leave you without showing you how much you mean to me. I love you, Amie. And you're the only witch for me."

Then he turned and left. I hugged myself and watched him go.

Maybe there was hope yet.

I just wish he'd said girl instead of witch.

Chapter 22

The next morning my anger was still there, right along with the pain and the beginnings of several bruises. Perhaps giving her three opportunities to land her punches and kicks hadn't been such a great idea after all. At least, that was what my body was telling me now. My brain, however, was still really happy with the final outcome of that tap out.

Now she knew exactly what I was capable of. And she had to know that Opie was my boyfriend. He was mine, dang it. And yes, I would fight for him. In my heart, that was what that fight had been about. Even if she hadn't known it at the time. If she had any brains, she should be able to figure it out.

I allowed myself a little extra time in bed, just wondering how to spend my day. I needed something to do to take my mind off things. Then an idea started forming in my head, and I felt a smile coming on.

If I could catch this killer before the sheriff and his gang did, that would pretty much seal my investigative reputation. And show little Miss Missy that I was truly a woman to be reckoned with on several levels. Maybe she had a nice little sheriff's department hat, but I had my own little career. I wasn't bound to the rules and regulations like she would be.

Okay, so maybe I was. But there were ways I could bend

things to suit my needs that an officer of the law couldn't. Not without major risk, anyway.

I figured they had their own line of reasoning on who the culprit was, and truthfully, I had absolutely no idea where to start even thinking about putting the blame. Who did it was a mystery to me still.

But even with that being the case, I had a place to start. The cigar club. Both deaths so far had somehow been tied to that place. Both men went there regularly. If it was a vigilante we were dealing with, that might just make the club itself a target. Or perhaps that was how he was picking his victims? Either way, staking out the club with any available time on my hands just sounded like a good idea.

This time, I'd be taking my bike. It would be a long ride in the heat, but it would be much easier to hide in the woods. I didn't want my car giving me away again.

Besides, I could use the exercise to loosen up my muscles. They needed it.

The only question now was what to do with my time until my planned stakeout tonight at the club.

When I walked out of my bedroom, the first thing I noticed was Mabel's note on the kitchen table and the lack of her bag by the couch.

I really appreciate you letting me stay here while I worked things out in my head, Amie. I'll be going home after work tonight. It's time to restart my life for good. Hopefully, you and the sheriff can catch whoever did this and make that a little easier for me too. Mabel.

Sure thing, Mabel. I'll do my best to make that happen.

Then I walked into my sitting room. What the...? Destiny had somehow managed to open my little cabinet that held my board game collection and had then dragged every last one of them out and onto the floor. Several of them had opened and game pieces and dice littered the floor.

"Destiny! What the blazes has gotten into you?"

It took me a minute to find her in all the mess. She was tiny, even for a kitten. When I finally located her, I could tell from her smug look that she wasn't in the least bit sorry for her actions. In fact, she looked quite proud of herself.

I glanced down at her frowning. "If this becomes the new normal, you'll be sleeping in a kennel at night. You know that, right?"

She hissed at me while slashing her tail back and forth. What the heck had gotten into my sweet little kitten?

Then she reached out one tiny little delicate paw and tapped the floor in front of her. Paying a bit more attention, I noticed that the box she was sitting on was my Scrabble game and in front of her were four letter tiles.

H-E-L-P.

I swooped her up, looking her over. "What's wrong, are you okay? Do I need to take you to the vet? What happened?"

See, here's the thing. Most people might think the spelling of a four-letter word was just a happy coincidence. I wasn't one of them. I knew that this was the Goddess' way of telling me something. Or rather asking me for something.

Destiny's tale was still slashing even as she meowed at me. Like that wasn't confusing as all get out. Then I realized I had kind of piled on the questions a little thick.

I took a deep breath and looked down at the kitten in my arms. First things first. "Are you okay?"

"Meow."

"Do I need to take you to the vet for some reason?"

Destiny threw her tale about with gusto. That was a definite no.

I looked at the tiles and then back to her. "So, what do you need help with?"

She squirmed, and I let her down. She ran over to the window that looked down into the backyard. I could see Billy already hard at work down there. With any luck, he would finish up the job today. Especially as it seemed he had a helper. Nancy was there too, handing him tools and even hammering in a nail or two.

I smiled looking down at them. Billy could be a good male influence in her life. She really needed one, and the Ravenswind household was strictly female. If you didn't count the occasional visit from the Minehearts or Opie.

Who I was still more than a little angry with by the way.

Destiny jumped up on the window sill, pressing her nose against the glass. "Meow."

"You want me to go help them?" It didn't really look like they needed help. To me, it looked like they were doing just fine all on their own.

"Meow." This one was more insistent.

I frowned at her. What did she want me to do? Then I shook my head and turned back to the bedroom to get dressed. No matter. I kind of had the feeling that maybe the Goddess was more like me than I'd ever imagined. It was quite possible she was making things up as she went along too.

Even if that were true, spending the morning with my potential new cousin wasn't such a bad idea. She needed to know that we all had her back here. If we had anything to say about it, her life would be far different from here on out.

The rest of the morning passed by in what seemed to be the blink of an eye. Nancy was rather shy around me at first, but after watching me and Billy tease each other for a half-hour or so, she got into the game of things. For those few short hours, she got to be a kid. It was encouraging to know that part of her hadn't died long ago. That happens sometimes when kids have it as hard as Nancy had.

I was kind of sad to see noon roll around and Opal come out with a platter of sandwiches and lemonade. As we ate, she announced that Billy and I would be on our own for the afternoon as she and Nancy were going to collect the girl's things from her school.

The cloud came down over Nancy and the change was startling. The little girl of the morning was gone, just like that.

After they left, Billy turned to me.

"Her dad getting killed was the best thing that could have happened to her, wasn't it?"

I thought for a minute. "I'd like to say so, Billy, but until things shake out, no one really knows if that will be the case. Opal is trying to become a foster parent so she can take her in for good, but that might not go through." I shrugged. "Not everyone in town approves of us, you know."

He frowned at me. "Then what will happen to her?"

"She'll go to another foster home or an orphanage somewhere. Hopefully, a good one. But what really needs to happen first is for the sheriff to catch her dad's killer. I don't think she'll be able to move on until that happens."

Billy took a deep breath. "I guess that's true with Mabel and Tommy too, isn't it? They can't really get on with their lives and be together until this is finished."

"I just hope that doesn't take too long."

He nodded, then turned back to the gazebo. "I just have to

do the trim work at the top now. That won't take long. I'll be done and out of your hair in a couple of hours."

"You're not in our hair, Billy. It's been kind of nice having you here." On an impulse, I reached over and hugged him. "Thanks for letting us help you this morning. I know you probably could have been done already if we'd just left you alone."

Billy blushed. "But I wouldn't have had near as much fun doing it."

I gave him a little extra squeeze and then let him go and headed back upstairs. If he really did get done soon, I might be able to use the meditation garden for a while this afternoon before I headed to the cigar club.

There was a definite feeling growing in my heart that I would need all the peace and strength I could get tonight.

Chapter 23

B illy was true to his word, and I got to be the very first one of us to use the meditation gazebo. It was absolutely perfect. Especially after I dragged my furry bean bag chair into the center of it.

After an hour of peace and quiet—and perhaps the smallest of naps—in my sanctuary, I felt strong enough to take on the world. Which was a very good thing, because tonight I was on my own.

Normally, I might call Opie to join me, but I wasn't quite ready to forgive him for last night yet. And my second choice of Ruby as a partner in staking out the club was a bust because she had dropped off Opal's car sometime last night and taken back off again with Arc. I had a feeling we would not be seeing much of her for a while. Not until the heat of passion cooled off a little.

With Ruby, that could take quite some time. She was a passionate kind of person.

Unfortunately, the fact that they were now a couple also took my third and final choice of a partner away too. My brother Arc.

So, yeah. I was doing this alone. And on my bicycle too.

Opal and Nancy must have returned while I was in my trance,

or sleep, whatever you want to call it. I called down to tell her I'd be going out for dinner. She didn't seem too upset about it. I think that was partly because her mind was dedicated right now to helping Nancy adjust to her new normal.

At least I hoped it was her new normal. The last thing in the world she needed right now was another change. Besides, I was beginning to think Opal needed her as much as she needed Opal.

I really didn't think there would be much need to get to the club before dark, as I just couldn't see the killer making a move in broad daylight. That hadn't been their way of doing things up to this point, and I couldn't think they'd go changing that now.

It would have helped if I'd known what I was looking for. Truthfully, all I was going on was a hunch and a growing feeling of dread in the pit of my stomach.

Something was going to happen tonight. Something big. And my witchy senses were telling me it would go down at the club.

As I still had a couple of hours before dark, I planned my trip so that I could stop in town for a bite to eat. Not Carney's, even though my stomach wasn't happy with me for that refusal. Instead, I went to the new chicken buffet and tried to temper down my appetite to that of a normal person. It wasn't easy, but I didn't want to be weighed down with a heavy meal.

Then I realized that Opie still had my binoculars from the day before. Crapsnackles. If I went by his place and asked for them back, he'd know where I was going. Plus, I wasn't ready to see him yet. He needed to stew in his own juices for a bit longer.

I ended up purchasing a cheap pair at the thrift store and

then pedaling my way the rest of the way to the club. It was a little farther out of town then I'd thought it was. I was getting soft with all the car usage. What I'd thought was only a mile or two ended up being almost triple that.

It was past hard dark when I finally leaned my bike against a tree and made my way to my stakeout spot. Or I least, I started in that direction. I had chosen a place for my bike off the beaten path. And I wasn't the only one that had done so.

When I spotted Billy Myers' truck, my heart sunk into the pit of my stomach.

Oh, Goddess, no. But my heart and brain were telling me yes.

When the hand landed on my shoulder, I almost screamed.

"You need to leave," Opie said. "Billy went in a few minutes ago and we're..." He stopped talking because the front door of the club opened and Billy came jogging out.

A red-haired female sheriff's deputy tackled him down to the ground. Opie pointed to the ground and then took off toward them.

Sod that. I ran after him.

Billy's eyes were wild when he saw me. "Run, Ms. Amie! Run! The bomb's gonna off in less than a minute!"

"Bomb?" And Opie and his dad were running all right, right into the building that was about to blow up.

I ran too. After them.

One thing with most witches is that to do a spell you need to prepare. Work out a rhyme, learn the finger manipulations, gather ingredients, all of that. That isn't so very true with Light Witches. Once we work a spell, or our power is used to fuel one worked by another, that spell becomes instantly available in a kind of spell bank.

As I ran through the threshold, I was making a withdrawal. I needed that Mineheart shield spell. But I needed to know where the blast would be coming from. Turning back to Billy, I yelled. "Where is it, Billy?"

From what I could tell he was crying but Missy shouted out. "He says it's in the cellar!"

Sheriff Taylor and Opie had the door yanked open in a heartbeat and after yelling a warning to the men down there, the great exodus began. Men came flooding past me, but I stood firm.

Until Opie saw me in the crowd. "Get out!"

I shook my head, drawing the spell out and into my arms and hands. It was almost here. It felt like the bomb's timer was matching my heartbeat. My hands went forward, and I screamed. "Everyone get behind me!"

The sheriff took one look at me and one quick glance at the door much farther away, and then he grabbed Opie and pulled him behind me, taking him to the floor.

Good thing too, because that's when the blast hit.

Chapter 24

I was trusting to the hope that this explosion would have much less force to it than the one at the warehouse had. There, I had the help of three very powerful Earth witches—well known for their protective powers. Now, it was just me. My life and the lives of my love, friend, and others depended on my power alone.

The thought was daunting. But not quite as daunting as the force from that single bomb's blast. It hit me like a ton of bricks. Knocking me and the ones behind me back by a good three feet.

But my shield held. Once the shock wave had passed, it got a trace easier to hold, but it was draining my magic fast.

"Get everyone out. I can't keep the fire back for long. This whole place is going to go."

I didn't have to tell the sheriff and Opie twice. They were already moving, running through the house and making sure it was clear. It seemed like forever before they were back at my side, even though the likelihood was it was a matter of a minute or two. Time stretched when you were holding back a force of this magnitude.

"Everyone's out." Sheriff Taylor had to shout to be heard over the roaring flames. "We've got to go."

I gave him a nod. "Go. I'll follow."

"The hell with that," Opie said. "Try to keep your concentration going for a few seconds longer." Then he scooped me up into his arms, and we were running for the door.

The flames took advantage of my movement, and even as we ran, they escaped from their under the floor prison, racing through the threshold of the basement stairwell as if they were intent on catching us.

Luckily, Opie was a little faster. Carrying me, that was no small feat.

He didn't stop until he was at the edge of the parking lot. Then he laid me down on the ground and looked up at his dad, who was still staring at me.

Oh yeah, he'd never witnessed my work up close and personal before. I was rather hoping he wouldn't make a big deal of it. News would travel pretty fast to the council if he did.

Not that it mattered at this point. In a decision between my future and Opie's life, I'd choose the latter every single time.

Instead of making an issue of it, he instead looked from me to the tree line that was altogether too close to the club.

"That fire is going to spread and, if we're not lucky, we're gonna have a wildfire on our hands. Anything you can do to stop that happening?"

I shook my head. "I'm too drained to make much of a difference. I need help."

His cell phone was out in a heartbeat. Opal was his first call, the fire department his second.

The man was smart.

Opal was smarter.

Several things happened in the next several minutes. Opal

arrived in tandem with Patricia Bluespring and working together, we held the flames from reaching the trees until the fire department arrived and got that side of the house, where the main blaze was centered, under control. It took a while.

By the end, the sheriff wasn't the only one giving me funny looks. Only this time it was a much more immediate threat to my well-being. Patricia was a council member.

Maybe Opal hadn't been so smart after all. Or maybe my magic had drained enough from the initial blast to make me appear a little more normal? That's what I was telling myself, anyway.

I just hoped it was true.

Sheriff Taylor took Billy Myers in to book him on double murder charges and a hell of an arson charge for starters. If there had been anyone downstairs that hadn't made it out, that would be tacked on to it too. I was so hoping that wasn't the case.

Opie, of course, stayed glued to my side.

When my mom and my new family arrived, I was given leave from the fight. By then it was mostly over, anyway. As I limped over to Opie's car, I looked over at him.

"How did you figure out it was Billie?" I asked. I mean, sure hindsight is one thing. It was pretty clear now, but before it hadn't been. Although I was kind of thinking this was what Destiny had been referring to with the cryptic help message. Not the building of the gazebo.

My bad.

"We didn't. Missy was staking out the club, and she saw Billy sneaking in and called us in. After that, it was pretty apparent. Before that, no clue." Then he gave me that lopsided smile of his. "Guess I shouldn't have admitted that, though, should I?

Let me change my response to your question. Awesome police work. That's what cracked the case wide open."

I glanced back at the dwindling fire. As hot as it had started, it was burning itself out pretty quickly. Especially with all the water and magic being thrown against it. The club was a goner for sure, but we'd survived.

That was all that really mattered at this point.

"I'll take that answer." Then I shivered. "Can I ask a favor?"

Opie's eyes traveled over to the fire too. We'd had a close call. There was no denying that.

I'd always known that Opie and his dad put their lives on the line for others on a daily basis. But watching them run into a building that they knew was about to explode? That had really put a lock on that knowledge. I wasn't handling it well.

This time, I'd been there. The next time I might not be so lucky.

"Right now, you could ask me anything, and, if it was in my power, it would be yours."

"Could you spend the night with me tonight?"

His breath caught as he jerked his eyes back to me. "I can so do that."

Chapter 25

If either of us had been expecting to take our relationship to the next level that night, we would have been disappointed. Luckily, we were both on the same page in that respect. Holding each other was enough.

At least at first. When we woke up the next morning, it was a different story. I'm not even sure who really initiated it. One minute I was just stretched out beside him, watching him sleep and the next minute, clothes were flying.

Okay, so maybe I was the initiator. I'm all right with that. The main point is, he didn't say no.

My magic even behaved itself, more or less. Right up until the end. At that crucial moment, the whole room lit up like the fourth of July. Talk about a physical representation of a feeling, but my magic pretty much nailed it.

After things settled back down, Opie—oops, Trevor—had declared it far too early to get up and face the day ahead. I had to agree with him. But while he fell almost instantly back asleep, I was still lying here thinking.

Mostly about Billy.

I felt heartfelt sorry for the man. Being subject to all the raving sermons from Crazy Al outside the library whenever he visited Mabel and then seeing her bruised body inside... well, it had just been too much for his simpler mind.

Billy Myers was a good man who'd just been trying to help the people he cared about get a better life than the one they'd currently been dealt. I could understand that. I hoped when the time rolled around, the judge and jury would focus on that fact and see to it that Billy got the help he needed. He didn't deserve to be thrown away in a prison for the rest of his life.

And, yes, I know what he did was wrong. Murder is never right. I'm just... conflicted on this one.

Opie started snoring softly, and I snuggled a little closer. Right this minute, life was practically perfect. If it wasn't for that niggling thought at the back of my brain, it would be. But time and again, my mind kept returning to the Goddess' words. Change was coming. She'd made it sound like a warning rather than an announcement of good things to come.

But just for today, I would push that niggling thought to one side and rest in the knowledge that whatever that change happened to be, the Ravenswind family and friends could handle it.

Just for today, that would be enough.

The End... For Now

The Gemstone Witches will be back soon in Home, Familiar, Home. Be sure to join my mailing list so you will be the first to know when it's available!

A Note From Belinda

Thank you so much for reading Un-Familiar Magic. I truly hope you enjoyed it! Please check out my website at BelindaWrites.com for updates on upcoming books.

Also, if you can spare a few minutes, please consider giving my book a review. I'd really appreciate knowing what you thought of it.

Belinda White
October 2019

Other Books by Belinda White

Accidental Familiar Series:
All Too Familiar
Relatively Familiar
Un-Familiar Magic

Benandanti Series:
Finders Weepers
Sister's Keepers
Demon Peepers

Printed in Great Britain
by Amazon